Dear Reader,

When the Temptation editors invited me to write the final two books in the Bachelor Arms series, I was thrilled. Of course I wanted to contribute to this series, with its legendary Hollywood mansion, its mysterious mirror, its colorful cast of characters and its delectable bachelor heroes.

Almost a decade has passed since I wrote my first Temptation. Lately, I've been busy writing for two of Harlequin's other lines—twenty-nine books for Harlequin American Romance, half a dozen for Superromance—but I've always loved writing fast-paced, sizzling-hot romances. "Fast-paced" and "sizzling-hot" describe *The Lady in the Mirror,* in which Clint McCreary, a cynical ex-cop from New York City, travels to Los Angeles in search of his runaway sister and instead finds the ghost in the mirror. He also finds Jessie Gale, a rescuer of lost souls, who sets out to save Clint when she realizes that he's haunted by ghosts of his own.

I'm an East Coast native who spent several years living in California, so I've always been intrigued by the culture clash between New York and Los Angeles. You might think that, given their widely divergent life-styles, hard-bitten Clint and sunshine-mellow Jessie will never be able to understand each other. But miracles can happen when love—and a ghost—get into the act!

You can write to me care of Harlequin Temptation.

Sincerely,

Judith

Judith Arnold
c/o Harlequin Temptation
225 Duncan Mill Road
Don Mills, Ontario M3B 3K9
Canada

BACHELOR ARMS

Come live and love in L.A. with the tenants of Bachelor Arms

Bachelor Arms is a trendy apartment building with some very colorful tenants. Meet three confirmed bachelors who are determined to stay single, until three very special women turn their lives upside down; college friends who reunite to plan a wedding; a cynical and sexy lawyer; a director who's renowned for his hedonistic life-style, and many more…including one very mysterious and legendary tenant. And while everyone tries to ignore the legend, every once in a while something strange happens….

Each of these fascinating people has a tale of success or failure, love or heartbreak. But their stories don't stay a secret for long in the hallways of Bachelor Arms.

Bachelor Arms is a captivating place, home to an eclectic group of neighbors. All of them have one thing in common, though—the feeling of community that is very much a part of living at Bachelor Arms.

BACHELOR ARMS

BACHELOR HUSBAND February 1995
Kate Hoffmann

THE STRONG SILENT TYPE March 1995
Kate Hoffmann

A HAPPILY UNMARRIED MAN April 1995
Kate Hoffmann

NEVER A BRIDE May 1995
JoAnn Ross

FOR RICHER OR POORER June 1995
JoAnn Ross

THREE GROOMS AND A WEDDING July 1995
JoAnn Ross

LOVERS AND STRANGERS August 1995
Candace Schuler

SEDUCED AND BETRAYED September 1995
Candace Schuler

PASSION AND SCANDAL October 1995
Candace Schuler

THE LADY IN THE MIRROR November 1995
Judith Arnold

TIMELESS LOVE December 1995
Judith Arnold

THE TENANTS OF BACHELOR ARMS

Ken Amberson: The odd superintendent who knows more than he admits about the legend of Bachelor Arms.

Eddie Cassidy: Local bartender at Flynn's next door. He's looking for his big break as a screenwriter.

Morgan Delacourt: He liked his isolation...until his fate was irrevocably twined with the Legend of Bachelor Arms.

Jill Foyle: This sexy, recently divorced interior designer moved to L.A. to begin a new life.

Natasha Kuryan: This elderly Russian-born femme fatale was a makeup artist to the stars of yesterday.

Clint McCreary: A cynical ex-cop who's looking for his runaway sister. Then he's back to New York where he belongs. But Bachelor Arms has its own effect on people....

Brenda Muir: Young, enthusiastic would-be actress who supports herself as a waitress.

Bobbie-Sue O'Hara: Brenda's best friend. She works as an actress and waitress but knows that real power lies on the other side of the camera.

Bob Robinson: This barfly seems to live at Flynn's and has an opinion about everyone and everything.

Theodore "Teddy" Smith: The resident Lothario—any new female in the building puts a sparkle in his eye.

THE LADY IN THE MIRROR

JUDITH ARNOLD

Harlequin Books

TORONTO • NEW YORK • LONDON
AMSTERDAM • PARIS • SYDNEY • HAMBURG
STOCKHOLM • ATHENS • TOKYO • MILAN
MADRID • WARSAW • BUDAPEST • AUCKLAND

To Ted, with love

ISBN 0-373-25661-2

THE LADY IN THE MIRROR

1

SHE DIDN'T LOOK like a hooker.

Steering his gaze from her, Clint scrutinized the three other girls on the corner. He knew the rule about not calling grown women girls, but the females in question couldn't be much past their midteens. Despite their outfits—short shorts, halter tops and high-heel sandals—they looked less like tarts than like children playing dress up. Their legs were skinny, their fannies nonexistent. Beneath their face paint they looked hungry and scared.

Los Angeles wasn't much different from New York, he decided. Fewer skyscrapers, palm and citrus trees instead of holly and pine, but a city was a city, and every city had its population of kids and runaways trying to survive on the streets. The biggest difference between New York and Los Angeles was that L.A. was a good forty degrees warmer, allowing its street kids to flaunt more flesh than the New York street kids who looked for business on the sidewalks connecting the Port Authority Bus Terminal to Times Square. When Clint had boarded the plane at LaGuardia yesterday morning, the raw November sleet had chilled his bones. Now the dry heat of Southern California was making him sweat.

Like the girls loitering on the corner of Sunset and Hill Street, the woman who stood with them was dressed for summer, if more modestly. Her floral print skirt fell past her knees, but when the sun filtered through the gauzy fabric Clint could see the silhouette of her long, slender legs. Her sleeveless blouse had a scooped neckline, but it covered everything it had to cover, leaving Clint to imagine the curves underneath. She looked strong and sturdy, her arms graceful and sun-bronzed, her hair woven into a thick blond braid that fell halfway down her back, her bottom round enough to fill a man's hands and her eyes blue enough to light up his soul.

The hell with that. She was standing with the others, no doubt in the market for some action just like the rest of them. If she looked older and less desperate, all it meant was that she was more successful than they were when it came to plying their trade.

Maybe she was the ringleader. The madam. Maybe Clint ought to be thinking the worst of her.

He scanned the girls once more. They were younger than his sister, but not by much. If she was hanging out on a street corner the way this trio was, dressed in skimpy rags . . . So help him, he was going to strangle the bastard she'd run off with, and then drag her home and lock her up somewhere safe.

If it wasn't already too late.

He cursed the anger and fear that gnawed at his gut. Thinking the worst was a shortcut to the devil's doorstep. Clint wasn't going to let himself contemplate the ghastly fates that might have befallen Diana since she'd dropped out of school, straddled the rear seat of her boyfriend's Harley-Davidson, and headed for L.A.

The tall, blond woman on the corner was talking to the young girls, listening to them and talking some more. One pointed at Clint where he sat behind the wheel of his rental car, which was temporarily parked in front of a bus stop.

The blond woman turned and frowned at him. If she was looking for business—either for herself or for her little pals—she would have been smiling invitingly. Her expression was about as close to a smile as this trashy downtown block was to the Garden of Eden.

Planting her fisted hands on her hips, she stormed across the sidewalk to his car. "What are you staring at?" she roared, leaning over to confront him through the open, passenger-side window.

The car filled with the faint scent of baby powder. The midday sun glazed the left half of the woman's face, emphasizing the sculpture of her cheeks, her narrow nose and her stubborn chin, and then drawing his attention to the sleek lines of her collarbone, and down farther to the hint of a shadow between her breasts, barely visible above the neckline of her blouse. He pictured her dusting her baby powder in that soft, feminine hollow. He pictured her choosing powder over some musk-based perfume because the sweet, fresh fragrance tapped into some strange male fantasy of innocence combined with lust.

He quickly erased the thought. "I'm staring at your friends," he said impassively.

"Well, put your eyes back in your head. They're not available."

"I'm not—"

"My advice to you, sir, is to move on. This neighborhood could do with a few less sleazeballs cruising for sex. And those girls—"

"I just want to talk to them," he said, refusing to let her hostility rile him. She had him wrong, more wrong than she could guess, but he wasn't going to let her put him on the defensive. "I'm looking for someone."

"I'll bet you are. Well, go look somewhere else. And while you're at it, look for someone your own age. And stay on the right side of the law, why don't you?"

He almost retorted that he was as legal as it got. But then it occurred to him that she might be, too. "Are you a cop?" he asked.

She chuckled. He wondered whether she was laughing at him, but there was nothing derisive in the sound. It was deep, throaty, oddly erotic. "No, I'm not. If you want to get arrested, though, I could arrange it for you."

"*I'm* a cop," he said, bending the truth a little. "And I'm looking for a girl named Diana McCreary. She's a runaway, and she's somewhere in L.A. I thought maybe those kids might have crossed paths with her."

The woman's smile changed. It seemed to rise through her face, losing strength around her mouth and gaining it in her eyes. They glowed, far bluer than the smog-tinged Southern California sky. "You're a cop? Why don't I know you? What precinct are you with?"

"I'm from New York City," he told her, not bothering to mention that he'd quit the force a couple of months ago. He was still in law enforcement; he'd only traded one end of the business for another. "I'm here as a civilian," he explained, stumbling onto the obvious reason a woman in her line would know a lot of cops. Given her natural beauty and feisty attitude, she probably had vice squads all over town under her thumb—or on her payroll.

"And you're looking for..." The woman frowned. "What did you say her name was?"

"Diana McCreary." From an inner pocket of his blazer he pulled a print of the snapshot he'd brought with him. It had been taken barely two months ago, the day his father and stepmother had driven Diana to Sarah Lawrence to begin her first year of college. Diana had looked radiant then, sure of herself, primed for adventure.

Who would have thought the adventure she'd wind up taking would be a cross-country jaunt with a tattooed, grunge rock wanna-be?

The woman reached into the car to take the photograph from Clint. Her fingernails were short and even, glossy with a clear lacquer. Her hands looked soft enough to pose for skin-cream ads. They sparked X-rated notions in Clint's mind, visions of her smooth, slender fingers trailing across his skin.

He hadn't traveled three thousand miles to indulge in adolescent fantasies about a streetwalker, no matter how much she resembled the California golden goddesses he and his friends used to dream about during their coming-of-age days on the streets of Jackson Heights. He had to stay focused on his mission: finding Diana and hauling her home.

The woman straightened up. "I'll be right back," she said, then carried the photo across the sidewalk to where the underage harem awaited her. The girls huddled around the photograph as the woman talked to them. They passed the picture around, shot quick, curious glances at Clint, and conferred among themselves.

After a minute, the woman returned to the car, bent down and rested her forearms on the chrome trim of the open window. "Nobody recognized her," she reported. She didn't sound resigned, though. Her smile was gone, but her eyes still glowed, clear and resolute. "When did she get into town?"

Clint stared at the photo, which the woman held in her left hand. It wouldn't be easy to take it from her without touching her wrist, her fingers, the smooth ridge of her knuckles. "Look," he said, his voice surprisingly gruff. "If none of your friends recognized her, I'll go ask around at some other hangouts."

"Just because these girls haven't seen her doesn't mean some of my other kids might not have. I'd like to show this picture to a few more of my people."

As attractive as the woman was, her words turned Clint off more effectively than a bucket of ice water dumped in his lap. Not only was she in charge of the hookers on this corner, but apparently the *lady* was managing an extensive operation.

"I can do a tour of the local street action myself, thanks," he snapped.

The woman seemed taken aback by his harsh tone. A scowl momentarily darkened her eyes, and then she laughed, that lush, throaty sound that turned him on all over again. "I run a program for runaway teenagers," she told him. "A shelter, counseling and support services. It's called Rainbow House. I've worked with hundreds of runaways. They're all my kids, Mr.... ?"

"McCreary," he said, properly chastened. This woman was a social worker, a professional do-gooder. "Clint McCreary."

The woman assessed him, then glanced at the photo again. "Is this girl your daughter?" she guessed, sounding uncertain.

"I'm not *that* old. She's my sister. Half sister, if you want to get technical about it."

The woman seemed pleased by that bit of information. "I'm Jessie Gale," she said, reaching across the seat to shake Clint's hand. Her skin felt even softer than it looked. He held her hand as long as he dared, then let go and reminded himself, for the zillionth time since he'd glimpsed her with the girls on the corner, that he didn't have time to waste on a pretty L.A. lady.

"And you're, what? With social services or something?"

"Rainbow House is a private agency," she told him. "We do get some funding from the city, and some from the state. But a lot of it also comes from private sources." She studied the photograph of Diana once more. "Your sister hasn't darkened our doorstep yet, but that doesn't mean she won't. Can I take this picture with me?"

Clint nodded. He'd brought two dozen copies of the snapshot to L.A. with him with the intention of passing it around as necessary.

As he watched Jessie Gale slide the photograph into a side pocket of her skirt, he realized that he had no proof she actually was who she said she was. "I'd like to stop by your Rainbow House and talk to the kids myself," he said, partly to test her and partly because it was true.

"No problem." When she lifted her hand from her pocket she was holding a small leather envelope, from which she withdrew a business card. "Here," she said, passing it to him. "That's the address and the phone number."

Clint studied the card. The words *Rainbow House* arched in a rainbow-hued semicircle across the white rectangle, with Jessica Gale, Executive Director printed in small green letters under the arch. The design—the entire concept of a shelter for runaways—struck Clint as a throwback to the sixties. If Jessie Gale handed him a daisy and intoned a chant about peace, love and harmony, he wouldn't be surprised.

Yet the ingenuousness of Jessie Gale's rainbow shelter, with her multicolored business cards, touched him in an unexpected way.

"What time should I drop by?" he asked.

She let out another husky laugh. "We're always open. Twenty-four hours a day. But if you come after 9:00 p.m., the night guard will give you a complete going over.

We're pretty strict. All late-night visitors get searched. Our motto is, hope for the best but prepare for the worst." She shrugged good-naturedly. "Where are you staying, Mr. McCreary? If I hear anything about your sister, I'll get in touch with you."

At the moment, he wasn't staying anywhere. He'd stumbled upon a motel last night, but it had been seedy, the carpet smelling of mildew and the bathroom infested with a much larger breed of cockroach than what he was used to back East. He'd checked out of the motel that morning, resentful about having to pay for even one night in such a hole. The trunk of his car currently held his bags, and he had no idea where he was going to park them or himself come nightfall.

"I haven't got an address," he told her.

"Well, when you do, let me know." She said it so casually, he felt guilty reading anything into it. And really, the only thing to read into it was her willingness to help him find Diana. She wasn't asking for his address so she could pay him a social call.

Yet he heard more than professional poise in her voice, more than mere concern over another runaway. He couldn't put his finger on what it was, but it was . . . something. Something that spoke to him in a personal way. Something that carried within it the certainty that she *could* help him, that he was worth helping, that peace, love and harmony were possible even though he knew damned well they weren't. It was almost as if Jessie Gale's words, her smile, her whole spirit wore all the shimmering colors of the rainbow.

That was a remarkably poetic thought, especially coming from Clint, who rated poetry on par with peace and love when it came to useful concepts. He chalked up his response to Jessie Gale as a product of jet lag, fatigue and worry. If Jessie could help him, he would be indebted to her. Period.

"I'll be back at my desk by about two," she said after a quick glance at her watch. "Hopefully with those girls in tow. They could use a good meal and a clean bed."

"Who couldn't?" Clint muttered with a weary smile. Not only was he running on too little sleep, but he hadn't eaten anything since an English muffin and a cup of burnt-tasting coffee at six-thirty that morning. He'd tried to remain in bed longer, but the mattress had been too soft for comfort, and besides, his internal clock was still set on East Coast time.

"So, you can try to catch me at Rainbow House this afternoon, or else leave a message. Meanwhile, I'll show your sister's photo around."

"Thanks."

He watched as she backed away from his open window and gave him a confident farewell smile. Clint smiled back. He continued to watch her as she pivoted and returned to the girls. They talked among themselves for a minute, and then Jessie ushered them around the corner and out of view.

He was sorely tempted to tail her, to see where she was taking the kids. Not that it would take a degree from John Jay College of Criminal Justice to figure that great mystery out. She was taking them to her shelter, the address of which appeared on the card she'd given him. Whatever detours she made first, whatever other corners she visited, whatever other runaways she roped in, sooner or later she was going to end up at the Rainbow House.

Sooner or later, he was going to end up there, too. But she'd said she wouldn't be at her desk until two o'clock. That gave him several hours to roam the city on his own, showing Diana's picture around, and questioning other street kids.

He was an ex-cop, with a cop's skills and instincts, he reminded himself as he revved the engine and eased into the flow of traffic on Sunset Boulevard. He didn't need a spirited blond social worker doing his job for him. He could find his sister—or at the very least, he could continue his search—without Jessie Gale and her enchanting smile getting in his way.

SHE KNEW THE TYPE. Hard-bitten, seen it all, trust nobody, trust nothing.

A cop.

She'd dealt with plenty of them in the past. They liked her, thought she was cute, appreciated her efforts but— bottom line—considered her a lunatic. Sure, they'd say, go out and save runaways if you want. The punks will only end up on some other block in a few months' time— or in a juvenile detention center. Or dead.

As if optimism were a curse. As if wanting to make the world a better place was the sort of dream only a fool would pursue.

She helped the last of her new charges into the van and slid the side door shut. She wasn't sure why Clint McCreary vexed her. He was just a guy, an out-of-towner trying to find his sister.

No, Clint McCreary wasn't just a guy. And she knew damned well why he vexed her.

His eyes.

She swallowed a small laugh. At twenty-seven, Jessie was savvy enough not to let a man get her all twisted up inside. That Clint McCreary had the most soulful, sexy, smoke gray eyes she'd ever seen was irrelevant. That those eyes were deep-set, and the skin at the outer edges was pleated from too much squinting or too much smiling—in his case, Jessie suspected it was the former—and when he looked at her she felt as if he were X-raying her mind as well as her body...

It didn't matter.

She would help him because it was her job to help runaways reconcile with their families when a reconciliation was possible. Sometimes it wasn't. Perhaps this Diana McCreary had run away from home because living at home was impossible for her.

Somehow, though, Jessie didn't think that was the case. For all the dark fire she'd seen in Clint's eyes, she'd detected no rage, no malice, none of the pathological clues that warned her against urging certain runaways to return to their families. The girl in the photograph looked happy and healthy. Jessie wanted to believe she came from a decent home.

Circling the van to climb in behind the wheel, she felt the photograph through the pocket of her skirt, the stiff rectangle tapping against her thigh. Having a picture of Clint's sister was almost like having a piece of him with her.

Behind her, she heard the quiet chatter of the three girls she'd talked into coming to the shelter for some food. She didn't know much about them, other than that they were hungry. Some kids opened up quickly, others not at all. After this group had something to eat, Jessie would ask Susan to try to pry some information from them: where they were from, how long they'd been on the streets, whether they were in the trade, whether they were doing drugs. Whether they'd be receptive to a little counseling, a little truce forging, a telephone call to their parents or guardians. Bit by bit, Jessie and her staff would give these girls what they gave all the runaways at Rainbow House: a chance to change direction, to go back home and make things right.

"What about my stuff?" one of the girls called forward.

Jessie peeked at her rearview mirror to determine who'd spoken. "What stuff?"

"I have some stuff. It's at a house in West Hollywood." Her voice rose tentatively at the end of the sentence, turning it into a question.

"I'll have Chuck get it for you," Jessie promised. "He's on my staff, and he's big. Nobody messes with him. He'll be able to get your stuff for you."

"Okay. It's, like, my Discman."

"Don't worry about it." After three years of working with troubled teenagers, Jessie was still mystified by the convoluted workings of their brains. Here was an underfed young girl, trying to eke out a living on the streets, and she was more worried about her CD player than her own safety.

Then again, that CD player might have been the only thing of value the girl had ever owned.

"They have good food at this place?" one of the other girls asked.

"Nothing fancy, but yeah, it's good."

This brought a cheer from Jessie's passengers. They resumed their conversation among themselves, freeing Jessie to think.

About Clint McCreary. About whether his sister was hungry, or homeless, or helpless. About why his eyes looked so much more rueful than those of the young lady in the photograph. Jessie visualized him as he'd appeared through the open window of his car. His lanky body had seemed shoehorned in behind the wheel, and he'd held himself calm but taut, as if ready to spring. He'd

been dressed for cooler weather, in jeans, an oxford shirt
and a blazer. His hair was as dark as his eyes, and much
too long. Evidently, his police department in New York
had a more lax grooming code than the LAPD.

She wondered what his hair would feel like if she
twined her fingers through the long, dark waves. Thick
and coarse, or silky?

A quiet laugh escaped her. Los Angeles was filled with
gorgeous men—most of whom were jerks, but even so,
she had no reason to let a grim, tense, absurdly virile-
looking East Coast cop hold her mind hostage.

She had to think about the three girls in the back seat,
and the ten kids currently in residence at Rainbow
House. She had to get herself psyched for her luncheon
meeting with the director of the Espinoza Fund, from
whom she was trying to wrangle a grant. She simply
couldn't let herself be sidetracked by the man with the
haunting gray eyes.

He was just another distraught relative looking for just
another runaway in L.A. Just another guy.

Sure, she scoffed to herself. And she was the Queen of
England.

BY FOUR IN THE AFTERNOON, Clint was exhausted. He'd
driven around the city, blasting the car's air conditioner
full force and muttering under his breath about the heat.
His jacket lay on the seat next to him. His shirtsleeves
were rolled up and his throat was parched.

He'd shown Diana's photograph all over town. Maybe
it was a good sign that no one had recognized her; at least
she hadn't become familiar to the panhandlers and crack-
heads who lined the sidewalks of derelict neighborhoods here, just as they did in New York. Less auspi-
cious was the fact that the clerks he'd shown Diana's

picture to in record stores and fast-food joints hadn't recognized her, either. She had to be somewhere; she'd called her mother twice last week, both times insisting she was in L.A. Diana was many things, but a liar wasn't one of them.

He'd paid a courtesy call at one of the precinct houses. The cops there greeted him warmly, just as the cops back home would greet a fellow officer from L.A. But as Clint had already known, they couldn't do much to help him unless he had a reasonable suspicion that Diana had been the victim of foul play. She was eighteen years old, of legal age, and those two phone calls to her mother denied him a justification for filing a missing-persons report. He left a copy of her photograph with the desk sergeant, anyway.

But no matter what he did, where he went, or whom he talked to, Jessie Gale remained a vivid presence in his mind. During his travels through the city, he'd been acutely conscious of the time, constantly performing the calculations: an hour and fifteen minutes until she would be back at her office. Forty minutes. Twenty-five.

When two o'clock finally arrived, however, he didn't go to Rainbow House. He couldn't shake the understanding that before he went to see her, he ought to have a place to stay. He told himself he wanted to be able to give her a phone number where she could reach him if she heard any news of his sister. But one small, idiotic part of him insisted that he had to have a room he could bring her to, a bed he could invite her to.

Absolutely insane. He wasn't going to bring Jessie Gale anywhere, invite her anywhere, or do anything that could be described in a single sentence containing the words *Jessie* and *bed*.

Even so, he was burdened by the knowledge that his bags were baking in the trunk of his car and he had nowhere to go after his tiring day. He had to find a motel—a clean, insect-free one. And he had to get something cold, and preferably alcoholic, to drink.

He cruised to the corner of Wilshire Boulevard, passing a massive pink mansion. The building seemed grand but faded, decked with wrought-iron terraces and landscaped with palms and squat shrubs. He wondered what artistic genius had decided to paint the eaves turquoise. He'd expected Hollywood to be garish and tacky, and this house fit the bill.

Shaking his head, he spotted a pleasant-looking eatery on the corner. A mint-condition Corvette pulled out of a parking space near the front door. Clint scooted his rental car into the space.

Climbing out, he groaned at the cramps in his legs and the stiffness of his neck. Too many hours behind the wheel, driving in this bizarre city of automobile addicts. Too many hours in a vehicle too small for a six-foot-tall man.

He let out a long breath, dug his thumbs into the knotted muscles at the nape of his neck, and glanced at the sign above the tavern's door. Flynn's. An Irish pub, just the thing. Clint would get a beer and a sandwich. He'd unwind, review his day's lack of progress and figure out a strategy for resuming tomorrow's search. Starting at Rainbow House.

But first he had to figure out where the hell he was going to spend the night.

2

"HOW'D IT GO?" Susan asked.

Jessie had already stepped out of her high-heel leather pumps. She padded in her stocking feet down the hall to her office, her shoes hooked over the fingers of her left hand and her portfolio tucked under her right elbow. "It went fine," she reported, crossing the threshold into her office and tossing the shoes into a corner of the small, plant-filled room.

"You were supposed to be back by two."

"I know." She dropped her portfolio onto her desk and shrugged out of the jacket of her linen suit. The casual skirt and blouse she'd had on that morning lay draped across the back of a chair, but she bypassed those for the jeans and T-shirt folded on a shelf in her closet. Since she spent so much time at the shelter, she kept plenty of spare clothing on hand for all occasions—including fancy luncheons. The suit she had on was one of two she stored in her closet.

She closed the door, shutting out the din of the television in the lounge, and let out a long sigh. "Did anybody stop by to see me?"

"Anybody?" Susan scowled, then grinned knowingly and flopped onto the worn love seat. "As in, a guy?"

Exactly. "As in anybody," Jessie said crisply, plucking the pins from her hair. The knot she'd twisted it into uncoiled into a crooked braid. She felt loose strands drizzle down around her cheeks and neck.

"Well, actually, a guy *did* drop by," Susan informed her.

She refused to let herself believe it might have been Clint McCreary—and she refused even more adamantly to acknowledge the shiver of hope that skipped down her spine at the possibility that he might have come. "Who?" she asked with all the nonchalance she could fake.

"Billy."

Jessie hid her disappointment. "Billy who?"

"Billy No-Last-Name. He claimed to be Laurie Steffano's boyfriend."

"What did Laurie have to say about it?"

"She told him her parents were wiring her the money to go back to Cleveland, and he could drop dead—or something to that effect."

"Good for Laurie." There was no such thing as an easy victory in Jessie's job. Each kid rescued was a triumph to savor. That fifteen-year-old Laurie Steffano had decided to put her dreams of showbiz stardom on hold and return home to finish high school qualified as a triumph of the highest order.

Jessie arranged her jacket on a hanger, pulled off the plain shell blouse she'd worn under it, and donned her T-shirt. She had promised herself a dozen times that she wasn't going to think about Clint McCreary any more. His missing sister, sure—Jessie would give Diana McCreary the same attention she gave any runaway. The young woman's picture was currently fastened to a bulletin board in the front hall, along with the shelter's schedules and a few other photographs of missing children. If anyone—runaways, police officers or any of Rainbow House's staff—spotted her on the street, they'd let Jessie know.

But Clint was nothing more to her than a concerned relative. The fact that he hadn't visited Rainbow House that afternoon proved that he had no interest in her.

Which was how it should be. Whatever interest she had in him deserved to be squelched.

"So, how come your luncheon lasted for four hours?" Susan inquired.

Jessie shimmied out of her skirt and nylons and into her jeans. She had no shyness about undressing in front of Susan, whom she had known since the day she'd entered the School of Social Work at the University of Wisconsin. They'd become close friends, and a year after Jessie had put together the funding and community support to open Rainbow House, she'd summoned Susan to join the enterprise. At the tail end of a lousy love affair, Susan had leapt at the opportunity to move to California and try something new. In the two years that she'd been at Rainbow House, she had become Jessie's indispensable second in command.

"While Dr. Figler and I were at the restaurant," Jessie related, "this gentleman came in, and Dr. Figler called him over and introduced him to me. He's on the board of directors of the Espinoza Fund—and, it turns out, he's also a honcho at MTV. He started talking about how so many starstruck kids pour into the city and drive everyone crazy looking for work, and if there was anything MTV could do to help Rainbow House get the starstruck kids out of their hair, he'd be most grateful. So, I told him that one thing MTV could do was write us a big check."

"You are shameless," Susan declared, sounding less reproachful than awed.

Jessie shrugged. She often joked that the main difference between her and the kids she helped was that while they panhandled on street corners, she panhandled in boardrooms. "How are the new arrivals doing?"

"We've got them all logged in," Susan reported. "Two of them didn't want to talk. They just wanted to watch soaps on TV. The third one let us pass her name along to the police. She swore her parents didn't give a damn about her, but I think she was just saying that. She and I chatted for over an hour. I've got a pile of notes." In her denim overalls, with her hair cropped in an unruly shag, Susan looked not much older than the kids she and Jessie counseled. "I gave all three of them the run of the kitchen, and they pigged out. I wonder when they last had a well-rounded meal."

"We'll feed and house the other two for a while, let them watch their soap operas and see what happens. A few good meals and they may start opening up."

Susan nodded. Her dark eyes narrowed, boring into Jessie. "So, who's the guy?"

Jessie busied herself arranging her skirt on a hanger. "What guy?"

"The guy you were hoping would stop by this afternoon."

"I wasn't hoping for anything," Jessie muttered, then bit her lip, aware that she'd all but admitted that there *was* a guy whose comings and goings mattered to her. She quickly covered by explaining, "He's a cop from New York, and he's looking for his missing sister. I ran into him on Sunset near the Civic Center this morning. I was just wondering whether he'd bothered to show up here. He told me he would."

"A cop from New York. Just your type." Susan wrinkled her nose. Like Jessie, she had endured the patronizing attitudes of some local policemen. Even when Rainbow House managed to deliver another runaway to her family, a few of Los Angeles's finest couldn't find it in them to recognize the good work Jessie and her staff did.

Jessie had gotten the sense that Clint McCreary was jaded. More than just the smoky shadows in his eyes had told her, more than the grim set of his mouth. It was his stillness, his reserve, *something* that implied a hollow deep in his heart.

And Jessie was a romantic fool, seeing faces in the clouds and spirits in the shadows. Whoever he was, whatever dwelled within his heart, his only significance to her was as a big brother searching for his sister.

"Wanna grab a bite?" Susan asked, pulling herself out of the overstuffed cushions of the sofa. "I'm starved."

"I had a huge lunch," Jessie fibbed. In truth, she'd only picked at her cobb salad. But if she admitted that her appetite was off, Susan would know something was bothering her.

And Jessie wasn't prepared to explain to Susan what it was. She wasn't prepared to explain it to herself.

"Why don't you go get some supper?" she suggested. "I want to have a look at your notes on our new guest."

Susan eyed her dubiously. "Are you okay?"

"Couldn't be better," Jessie insisted, grinning. "I just wrangled a promise for a ten-thousand-dollar grant from the Espinoza Fund. Plus I've got an appointment at MTV for next week."

Susan clearly wasn't persuaded. "Whatever you say. I think I'll just grab some takeout and bring it back, so we can keep an eye on those other two girls you brought in. I'll bring you a burger or something, too."

"Thanks." If Jessie was the unofficial mother of the city's street kids, Susan was the unofficial mother of Jessie, fussing over her and feeding her as if she weren't capable of taking care of herself. But just as Jessie had a will of steel when it came to her charges, Susan had a will of steel when it came to Jessie. Arguing over a hamburger would only be a waste of energy.

Pleased that Jessie was accepting her heavy-handed nurturing, Susan moved to the door and swung it open. "And while we're eating," she said, backing into the hall, "you can fill me in some more about the cop from New York."

Before Jessie could tell her to stuff it, Susan was gone.

"A GHOST?" Clint blurted out.

"Sure," said the fellow sitting on the stool next to him. He'd introduced himself as Bob, and if he had an on-off switch Clint couldn't guess where it was. He yammered nonstop about the late-autumn drought, the Rams' inept defense, and the most recent price war among the major airlines.

Still, he was an entertaining guy to share a beer and a bowl of pretzels with. For a few precious minutes, Clint could forget about his missing sister and the hot, sprawling city he was searching. He could relax in this sleek tavern—not the neighborhood Irish pub he'd been expecting, but a stylish taproom furnished in dark wood, black tile and brass, the walls decorated with framed photos of matinee idols of yesteryear. Apparently, Flynn's was named after Errol Flynn, if the number of pictures of him on display meant anything.

"That's the legend," Clint's new buddy confided before popping a pretzel into his mouth. "I'm not making this up, you know. I couldn't make it up if I wanted to. According to the legend, the ghost lives inside a mirror—"

"Whoa." Laughing, Clint shook his head. It didn't matter that Bob was well dressed and friendly. He was obviously rowing with one oar out of the water. "It lives in a mirror?"

"Well, not everybody sees her. But if you do see her, they say either your greatest hope or your greatest fear will come true."

"Your greatest hope or your greatest fear." Clint pretended to give this his solemn consideration. "Not both?"

"Nope. One or the other. Isn't that right, Eddie?"

The bartender had been rinsing ashtrays at a sink behind the bar, but at Bob's summons he sauntered over. Obviously, he'd been listening to Bob's lecture on the supposedly haunted pink mansion next door. He probably wanted to see how far Bob would take it, and how much shinola Clint would swallow before he started to gag.

He glanced at Clint's beer bottle and determined it wasn't empty enough to replace with a fresh one. To be useful, he topped off the bowl of pretzels. "Are you bending this poor guy's ear, Bob?" he chided.

"Just telling him the truth about Bachelor Arms. You know, the ghost in the mirror. Back me up, Eddie. Tell him it's the truth."

"It's just a story," Eddie said.

Receiving scant support from the bartender, Bob turned back to Clint. "The way I heard it, someone was once murdered at Bachelor Arms. A Hollywood starlet. We're talking years ago, the twenties. Actors were always in and out of the mansion, tearing the place up, making whoopee, if you catch my drift. They say a cute young thing wound up dead after one of those orgies."

Clint eyed his companion with amusement. "This sounds like the plot of a bad movie."

"Movies aren't my line. You want to talk movies, you talk to Eddie." He gestured toward the bartender, who had finished washing the ashtrays and was now toweling and stacking them. "Eddie Cassidy, the world's greatest screenwriter, eh? What's the status of your latest epic, Eddie?"

The bartender shrugged diffidently. "Xanadu renewed the option for another three months," he said. "Whatever the hell that means."

"It means money in your pocket, that's what it means. What's the name of that masterpiece, again?"

"They keep changing the name. Last I heard, they wanted to call it *Tight Corners*."

"I like that." Bob nodded his approval. "It's got pizzazz. What do you think about *Tight Corners*?" he asked Clint.

Clint took a sip of beer and smiled. "Sounds good to me."

"I tell you, everybody's a star. You come to town looking for stardom?"

"No." Bob had inadvertently reminded Clint of why he *had* come to town. He didn't have time to make small talk with this yak-meister. "You wouldn't by any chance know of a motel in the area?" he asked. He would be able to take a spin around the city at night, checking out some rock clubs in search of Diana and her scuzzy boyfriend, but first he had to book himself a room.

"You looking for a place to stay?" Bob asked.

"A clean place," Clint emphasized. "One that doesn't have cockroaches."

Bob chuckled. "Bet you wouldn't find too many bugs at the Beverly Hills Hotel."

"A place that isn't going to bankrupt me," Clint clarified, smiling tolerantly although Bob was beginning to irritate him. The guy meant well enough; he just talked too much.

"Sure, there's probably something reasonably priced in these parts. One of the chain motels . . ."

"You could move into 1-G," a sultry alto drawl arose from somewhere behind Clint.

He spun on his stool and found himself staring at a strikingly pretty waitress. Blond hair, blue eyes . . .

A memory of Jessie Gale flashed across his mind.

He reminded himself that pretty women with blond hair and blue eyes were evidently a dime a dozen in Southern California. That had been the myth that had flourished in his hormone-driven adolescence, a myth reinforced by the pretty blond-haired, blue-eyed Heather Locklear types who populated countless television shows coming out of Hollywood in those days. This waitress fit the type: she had curves in all the right places, her features were neat and well proportioned, and her attire had a cheap-chic look to it.

But she wasn't Jessie Gale. Her eyes didn't shimmer with optimism. Her smile didn't reach inside him and squeeze. She looked cool and calm and guarded.

"What's 1-G?" he asked. It didn't sound like any motel chain he'd ever heard of.

Setting her tray down on the bar, the waitress gave a practiced flick of her head to send her hair back from her face. "I need two Beck's dark," she told the bartender, then turned back to Clint. "One-G is an apartment at Bachelor Arms. The one with the mirror in it."

"The mirror with the ghost?"

She nodded. "A man moved in last week. He got all his furniture arranged, got his phone hooked up . . . and then I reckon he saw the ghost, because he was gone in a nanosecond. He left behind everything but his toiletries. The landlord's trying to find someone to pick up the lease."

Clint swallowed a laugh. These folks were another species altogether. "I'm not looking for a lease," he said. "I'm only going to be in town a couple of weeks." He hoped finding Diana wouldn't take longer than that.

"Ken would be thrilled to get two weeks' rent out of someone. *Dark*," she repeated to the bartender when he put two regular beers on her tray.

Clint contemplated the wisdom of continuing the conversation and decided to let it run its course. "Who's Ken?"

"The landlord. Ken Amberson. He's spooky, but then, that's Bachelor Arms for you. I live there myself. And I know 1-G is unoccupied, full of furniture. You could probably negotiate yourself a sweet deal."

Clint regarded the waitress curiously. "You live there?" At her nod, he asked, "Have you seen this ghost?"

She gave him a saucy smile. "If I did, sugar, I wouldn't tell you." With that, she lifted the tray and waltzed off to serve her customers.

His gaze followed her while his mind veered in its own direction. He didn't believe in much of anything—and he certainly didn't believe in ghosts. What kept him from leaping off the stool and racing next door to inquire about the empty apartment were the details, the practicalities. For instance, cost. He hadn't yet finished the paperwork to formalize his new job—he'd been working out of the D.A.'s office, but only as an intern pending his passing of the bar exam. Just before he'd left for California he'd gotten the word that he passed. But even after his job became permanent, with a title and some status, he was never going to be a rich fat-cat lawyer.

He didn't want to be a rich fat-cat lawyer. He wanted only to get thugs off the streets and behind bars. A noble undertaking, but one that didn't pay enough for him to rent an apartment in this pleasant middle-class neighborhood of Los Angeles while he was still paying the rent on his apartment in Manhattan.

On the other hand, a furnished apartment would be nicer than a motel room. He'd have space to move, a kitchen, windows that overlooked more than a crowded parking lot or an even more crowded swimming pool . . . and a mirror with a ghost in it.

Yeah, sure. Like he could really buy into the loony-tune yarns of these Southern California people. Too much sun, he thought. Too much heat in the winter, and all that La-La-Land glitz, and the next thing you knew, these people were believing in ghosts.

What the heck. It wouldn't hurt to talk to the landlord. The worst that could happen was, the guy would quote a price in the stratosphere and Clint would go back to looking for a clean motel.

"Quite an eyeful, isn't she?" Bob murmured appreciatively.

Clint realized he was still staring after the waitress. Her appearance hadn't registered on him, though. What he'd been viewing, in the privacy of his imagination, was Jessie Gale paying him that social call, feeling comfortable because where he lived comprised more than a small room with a big bed. She could visit, he could entertain her, they could sit on the haunted furniture in the haunted apartment . . . and the bed would be waiting for them if needed.

Cripes. He wasn't going to take Jessie Gale to bed. He was going to ask her to help him find his sister, that was all. He didn't need a furnished apartment for that.

Yet as he rose from his stool and slid a few bills from his wallet to cover his beer, as he bade farewell to Bob the motor mouth and Eddie the screenwriter-bartender, as he strolled out of Flynn's and down the sidewalk to the pastel mansion next door, his thoughts circled round and round the idea of bringing Jessie to his place and letting her fill his temporary home with her energy, her optimism, her husky, sexy laughter. If, even if his mission to find his sister failed, he did get Jessie into his bed, this trip wouldn't be a total loss.

IT WAS THE UGLIEST mirror he'd ever seen.

It was enormous, dominating most of one living room wall, and framed in an elaborate mess of gray metal molded into swirly-curly shapes. If Clint were a ghost, he sure as hell wouldn't want to live in it.

The rest of the furniture suited him well enough. The previous tenant had left behind a sparse arrangement of sturdy, undistinguished sofas and tables, a faded rug on the floor, a small table and two chairs for intimate dining, and a broad brass bed for intimate whatever.

"I've got to tell you, I'm kinda leery about renting this place," the short, bald man who'd introduced himself as Ken Amberson warned him. "I mean, what with the last tenant taking a powder on me—"

"I don't believe in ghosts," Clint declared, studying the mirror with an intensity that would have amazed him if he'd given it any thought.

"I mean, if I had something else to show you—"

"I don't want something else. I want a place to live for a couple of weeks. With furniture. It's either this or a hotel. One month's rent on this place comes out a lot cheaper than a month at the daily rate in most hotels."

"Yeah, but—"

"And if you want to show the apartment to prospective tenants, I don't have a problem with that. Face it, Mr. Amberson, this works well for both of us." Damn, if it wasn't the most hideous mirror in the world. Staring at his reflection, Clint could see a combination of amusement and revulsion in his face. He could also see a five-o'clock shadow darkening his jaw, and wrinkles rumpling the cotton of his shirt, and weariness dulling his eyes.

One thing he couldn't see was a ghost.

"It's something, isn't it," Ken Amberson said, running his fingers over the bald crown of his head.

"Yeah, something else," Clint muttered.

"Yeah, it is, isn't it," Ken said reverently. "It was here long before I took over the building."

"Do you own the building?"

"Um . . ." Amberson fidgeted some more, his fingers scrambling over his scalp and then snagging on his earlobe. "I manage the building. There's some question on the ownership. It's a trust or something, a bank holds the title. Don't ask me. All I know is, I manage the place."

Clint turned from the mirror. "Do you believe that crap about the ghost?" It occurred to him that, given Amberson's diminutive stature—the guy couldn't be more than five foot five or six—he might have had to stand on a chair to look into the mirror properly.

The landlord peered up at him. "I've never seen it. But there's folks that say they have—and nothing good's come of it."

"The people at the bar next door tell me it can make your greatest hope come true."

"Or your greatest fear. Which is to say, Mr. McCreary, that more times than not, our greatest hope is something we ought to fear. You know what they say—

'Be careful what you hope for, because you just might get it.'"

Clint's greatest hope was that he would find Diana, and she would be safe and sound. His greatest fear, as far as he could guess, was that he wouldn't find her, or she wouldn't be safe and sound. He would allow himself no fears, no hopes, beyond that.

"I don't believe in ghosts, Mr. Amberson. Can we come to terms on this apartment?"

"You sure you want it? I've got the previous tenant's security deposit to cover this month, and . . ."

"I'm offering you one month's rent. Yes or no?"

"Well, if you really want it . . ."

Clint thought he'd made it quite clear that he really wanted it. He wasn't going to drop to his knees and beg. There was no need to haggle. All that remained was to sign a contract and write out a check, and then Clint could kick the landlord out, dive across that wide, soft bed and catch a few Zs without having to worry about an army of gargantuan cockroaches staging a dress parade from the kitchen to the bathroom.

"Let's get this deal done," he said briskly, tugging a pen from the inner pocket of his blazer.

A few minutes later, he closed the door behind Mr. Amberson's retreating form and sank into the nearest overstuffed chair. Apparently, the California way of doing things was indirectly, accompanied by an abundance of idle chatter. The only normal conversation he'd had all day had been with that desk sergeant downtown, who'd told him what he already knew: that he would have to verify Diana was officially a missing person before the cops could step in and help him search for her.

Clint was going to have to learn to deal with Southern Californians on their level. They were now his neighbors, and if they moved a little slower than New Yorkers did, if they approached life in a more leisurely fashion, he was simply going to have to adapt to their rhythms.

It was only temporary, anyway. He would put in his time and find his sister, and then he'd go back to New York, where winter felt like winter and people never walked when they could run. He would go back to the crowded streets, the noisy buses, a city where the closest thing to an earthquake was when a subway train streaked through a tunnel under his feet and made the sidewalk vibrate. He would go back to sleet and gray skies and leafless trees and know he was home.

Sighing, he slid off his jacket and tossed it onto the cushion beside him. A small white rectangle fell out of a pocket and onto the rug. Bending over, he saw the rainbow arch and the green lettering.

All right. Maybe Los Angeles had some things going for it, after all.

He picked up Jessie Gale's card and crossed the room to a small writing table near one of the large, grilled windows that overlooked a courtyard planted with bright tropical flowers. It felt all wrong to him to be viewing such colorful foliage in November.

It felt all wrong for him to be wishing he could step outside and pluck a few of those red blossoms, and bring them to a woman he'd barely met, whom he couldn't seem to get out of his mind.

He put down her card and turned from the window. Something caught his eye—a flicker of light in the mirror. The lamp by the sofa was bouncing its light off the reflective surface.

He strode back across the room to switch off the lamp—but halfway to his destination he noticed another flicker in the mirror, dark this time. A shadow. Moving.

His own shadow, he told himself. His own movement.

But he wasn't convinced.

He prowled toward to the mirror, cautious, silent, the way he used to tail a suspect during his days on the police force. His old instincts twitched to life; he instinctively reached under his left arm, groping for the shoulder holster he no longer wore. His hand flexed; he was frustrated to find himself without a service revolver to draw.

He discerned a movement in the mirror again, but it wasn't his own. He stood absolutely motionless, staring at the grotesque mirror and frowning as the reflection of the living room grew dim, losing focus.

Through a veil of fog he saw a woman dressed in white. Her pale face, framed in long black hair, appeared blurry at first but gradually evolved into a clear, fragile image. Her eyes were incredibly dark, two black holes sucking him in.

She smiled, a faint, enigmatic smile that seemed to say, *I know your hopes and fears. I know.*

Her lips curved into a more emphatic smile, not quite kind, not quite mocking. And suddenly she was gone. The room's mirror image was once more clear in the glass.

Clint let out a long sigh and realized, only then, that he'd been holding his breath for the endless minute that he and the figure in the mirror had exchanged gazes. As his lungs came back to life, so did his mind, rampaging through thoughts like a stampeding elephant, knocking notions over, crushing them.

He hadn't seen anything. He'd only hallucinated the woman in the mirror.

Or there was a real, flesh-and-blood woman in the room. Right this minute she was hiding somewhere, behind the curtain, in the kitchen, *somewhere*.

Or the mirror was actually a one-way reflector, and some local woman—perhaps in cahoots with Amberson—was standing on the opposite side of the wall, peering through the glass and pulling his leg, maybe trying to scare him off for some reason.

Or jet lag had belatedly made him delirious.

Or the stressful events of the last few months—Diana's graduation from high school, his own from Fordham Law, his cramming for the bar exam, Diana's departure for college, her absconding with her scumbag boyfriend—had all conspired to make him susceptible to California looniness.

Or...

There really was a ghost in the mirror.

Clint had seen her. And she'd seen him. She'd looked at him, looked *through* him, and smiled.

In thirty years of hard living, he had never experienced a moment's madness. He'd suffered terrible losses, he had his scars. But even at his absolute lowest point, he'd never been crazy.

Either he was crazy now, or someone was playing a trick on him...or a ghost lived in the mirror of the apartment he'd just rented. Option one: he'd return to New York in a straitjacket. Option two: he'd find out who had tricked him and what they were after.

Option three: his greatest hope—or, God help him, his greatest fear—would come true.

3

HE WAS WAITING FOR HER when she arrived at Rainbow House the following morning.

It was barely eight o'clock, earlier than she usually showed up for work. But she'd had a restless night, and she didn't feel like moping around her apartment when she could be getting things done at her desk. She had, in fact, considered taking the overnight shift at the shelter. But she'd decided a change of scenery might improve her spirits, so she'd gone home, leaving the staff bedroom to one of the two dozen volunteers—professional social workers and graduate students—who took turns spending a night at the shelter, keeping an eye on the kids.

The change of scenery *hadn't* improved her spirits. It wasn't the first thing she'd ever been wrong about, and it wouldn't be the last. She'd been wrong about Clint McCreary, thinking he had more on his mind than his missing sister—and that whatever that *more* was, it somehow involved Jessie. She'd been wrong to think he would make an effort to see her. She'd been wrong to waste any mental energy on him—although where her thoughts lodged seemed beyond her control.

No matter what she did last night—leafing through a magazine, watching a documentary about whales on TV, going through her grocery store coupons and throwing out the expired ones—her mind returned like a homing pigeon to the cop from New York City. She could think of no logical reason for this. He wasn't the only good-looking man in the world, and certainly not the *most* good-looking. His behavior hadn't been at all receptive to her; his attitude had been cool, reserved, almost gruff. That he cared about his half sister didn't mean much. Lots of people cared about their siblings. Jessie certainly cared about hers.

Yet long after she'd crawled into bed and turned off her bedside lamp, visions of Clint McCreary played across her imagination. She recalled his gray eyes, his smoky voice, the way his hair curled over the collar of his shirt in back. She recalled his long, blunt fingers, his harsh chin, his thin, sensuous lips.

What she needed was a fling. A warm body next to her in bed. She had her share of dates, but she hadn't been in a serious relationship since Danny had moved to Oregon over a year ago, disgusted with the city and with Jessie's insistence that the city was exactly where she was needed most. For a while she'd missed him, for a while she'd been heartbroken. But now...

Now, she was probably just lonely. And Clint McCreary was an intriguing place to park her fantasies.

He was also wrong for her. She was wrong to let him hijack her brain. Most of all, she was wrong to think he'd accept her invitation to contact her.

The following morning, as she entered the sprawling Victorian-style boardinghouse that she'd converted into a shelter for runaway youths, she discovered she'd been wrong again. Clint had come, after all.

He stood near the doorway to the television lounge, inspecting the bulletin board. His sister's photograph was still on display, along with snapshots of other missing youngsters. In addition to the photos, the board held work assignments—everyone living at the shelter had chores—counseling schedules, information on drug abuse programs and an array of bus and train time-tables.

From the front door, Jessie viewed only his back, yet she knew right away that the tall, lean man with the coal black hair and the long legs was Clint. Although she'd seen him only once, all folded up behind the wheel of a car that had seemed too small for him, she knew. Even if she'd had her eyes closed she would have known he was there. She felt his presence in her nervous system, in her gut, in her scalp and her toes and the center of her soul.

"Good morning," she said, regretting that she'd dressed in faded jeans and a Hard Rock Cafe T-shirt instead of something a little prettier. When she'd left her apartment that morning, she hadn't been in a pretty mood.

He spun around and smiled. He, too, was clad in jeans. Softly faded, they hugged his narrow hips and hinted at the athletic contours of his thighs and calves. A thick leather belt underlined his waist, drawing her attention back to his hips.

Definitely, she needed a new man in her life. Not Clint, but someone who loved Southern California the way she did, and didn't mind her erratic hours and her commitment to her runaways, and who was as open and affectionate as she was.

She steered her eyes upward. He had on an oxford shirt with the sleeves rolled up to his elbows. In his hand he clutched his blazer. He had long fingers, thick knuckles. Strong but surprisingly graceful wrists.

When her gaze met his, his smile waned slightly. A dimple creased one cheek, but his eyes were a lightless, troubled gray as he crossed from the bulletin board to the entry where she stood. She could guess he hadn't located his sister—if he had, he wouldn't have come to Rainbow House.

"Good morning," he said.

"You're here mighty early." Or else very late, she thought wryly. She had expected him to stop by yesterday afternoon.

"I still haven't got my time zones straight," he explained, then hesitated, as if sorting his thoughts. "Can you spare a few minutes?"

Jessie's impulse was to shout that she could spare as much time as Clint wanted. But of course she couldn't. She had work to do, clients to counsel, budgets to wrestle with and a staff to oversee.

Clients, budgets and staff could wait, though. And sparing her time for Clint *was* work. He had come to talk about his missing sister, nothing more. "Let's get some coffee and go to my office," she suggested.

He concurred with a nod. His mouth held its tenuous half smile and his eyes remained stormy.

She walked through the entry to the lounge and peered in. Last night's volunteer, a chunky redheaded student at the nearby university's school for social work, sat watching "Good Morning America" with two of the shelter's residents. "I'm here, Lynn," Jessie called out.

Lynn blinked at her and yawned. "Oh, hi, Jessie. I guess I'll be heading for home, then." She stood, stretched, and lifted her backpack from the floor at her feet.

"Anything happen last night?"

"No. It was real quiet. Those new girls got kind of chatty. They refused to tell me where they were from, but they're beginning to warm up. You might have a breakthrough with them today."

"Thanks." Jessie patted Lynn on the shoulder, then gestured for Clint to follow her down the hall.

The thumping beat of rap music assailed them as they neared the spacious kitchen at the rear of the house. Two boys currently in residence were preparing breakfast and jiving to the rhythm that drummed through the speakers of a boom box on one of the stainless-steel counters. "Turn it down a decibel," Jessie shouted above the noise.

One of the boys sent her a good-natured grin. In his baggy shorts and with his baseball cap turned backward, he looked less like a chef than like a sidewalk surfer as he stirred a huge pot of oatmeal on the six-burner industrial stove. "Hey, man, we need our music," he protested. "Can't do no cooking without a backbeat."

"You can cook with a quieter backbeat, Victor," Jessie shot back, glancing into the caldron of cereal on her way to the coffeemaker. "And don't forget to put a little brown sugar in there. Nobody'll eat it if you don't."

"Brown sugar don't make no difference. This stuff tastes like—" He caught himself before resorting to profanity, and gave Jessie another boyish grin. "Tastes like cow droppings, man."

"Yeah?" his helper, Tom, called from the counter, where he was mixing a pitcher of orange juice. "How would you know?"

"This stuff tastes like what you got growing between your toes." Victor stirred the oatmeal with a flourish.

"Put a little brown sugar in it," Jessie advised, "and it'll taste like oatmeal."

"I don't know why you make me cook this stuff," Victor complained. "Cooking ain't no man's work. You oughtta get one of the chicks to do this."

Jessie chuckled. "And what would you do while she was cooking?"

"I'd give her directions, tell her what to do, you know? I could be the boss."

"You ought to make that cereal a little thicker, like cement," Jessie teased. "Then we could use it to glue your mouth shut." She pulled two mugs from a shelf and turned to Clint. "Milk and sugar?"

He'd been watching her playful exchange with Victor from the doorway. He looked, if anything, even more bemused than before. "Black, please."

"Black it is." She filled the two mugs, added a splash of milk to hers, and carried them from the kitchen, offering a parting shot to Victor as she passed him: "Brown sugar. That's the secret. And *I'm* the boss. Not you, *me*."

"Yes, Wizard," he muttered, still grinning.

Clint said nothing as she led him to her office. After unlocking the door, she peeked in and grimaced at the fast-food wrappers and empty soda cans she and Susan had left on her desk last night. There was no way to tidy up the room without Clint's noticing, so Jessie bravely marched in, gathered the trash and dumped it into her wastebasket. Then she gestured toward the couch.

As soon as he started toward it, she realized she didn't want to sit behind her desk as if this were some sort of interview. Yet to share the couch with him would presume an intimacy that didn't exist. She was used to weighing such subtleties with her clients; sensitive, overwrought teenagers could be thrown seriously out of whack if things weren't arranged just right.

Clint wasn't a teenager. And if anyone was being too sensitive, it was Jessie. Suppressing another grimace at her foolishness, she wheeled her chair around from behind the desk and sat on it, facing Clint with the scuffed coffee table between them.

He gazed around the small room as he sat, his eyes lingering on a colorful framed poster of the Beach Boys, early vintage. "Fun, Fun, Fun!" was printed below their cherubic faces. It was the closest thing to an antique that Jessie owned, and it was quintessentially Southern California. It actually provoked a laugh from Clint.

As soon as the dark, husky sound slipped past his lips he grew somber again, his gaze skittering from the poster and landing on Jessie. He lowered himself onto the faded cushions of the sofa, cautious and wary, and stared at her over his cup of coffee as he sipped.

"So," she said, ordering herself to relax. "What can I do for you?" She knew the answer: she could find his sister. Yet the thought of jumping right into business depressed her. She wanted him to say something personal first.

And she had no right to want that.

"Why did that kid call you Wizard?" he asked. His voice was low, gravelly, stroking her nerve endings.

New York Cop, she reminded herself. He wasn't her type; she mustn't respond to his sexy baritone, or to his dark, disturbing eyes, or to his lanky physique. "A lot of the kids call me Wizard," she told him. "This is Rainbow House and my last name is Gale, like Dorothy Gale in *The Wizard of Oz.*"

"Oh. Of course." He seemed both amused and annoyed with himself for having failed to make the connection. "You named this place Rainbow House because your last name was Gale?"

"Not exactly. The building used to be a boardinghouse. Then it did time as a frat house, and then it was just a residence for a bunch of university students. Back in the early seventies, someone painted a rainbow on the roof. Anyway, the place was falling apart, and the owner needed a tax loss or something, so he sold it to us for one dollar. The building needed tons of repair, including a new roof. So we lost our rainbow. The name stuck, though. When people realized how my name fit into it, they started calling me Wizard, or sometimes just plain Oz."

"Who is this 'we'?"

"The board of directors."

He looked around once more, lingering for a moment on her desk, the pile of file folders, the outdated personal computer a benefactor had donated a few years back. "You have a board of directors," he half asked.

"Mostly for raising funds. Each board member can hit up his friends and business associates. It gives us a lot more access to money."

Clint nodded and sipped his coffee. Jessie waited for him to ask another question, or to broach the subject of his sister. All he did, though, was to lower his mug to the coffee table and rearrange his legs, spreading them and resting his elbows on his knees. He regarded her enigmatically.

"Are you okay?" she finally asked. It was much too personal a question, but he seemed perplexed, even anxious, and she felt compelled to do something about it. Making things better had always been her central motivating force. When she'd been a child, she would adopt every stray kitten and every injured bird she came across. She would negotiate truces between quarreling classmates and comfort her siblings when they were upset. When she'd decided to become a social worker, no one who knew her had been the least bit surprised.

Now she wanted to comfort Clint. Something was troubling him. He appeared to be in turmoil, and she wanted to make things right.

His immediate reaction to her question told her he didn't want her comfort. His eyes grew cold; his smile faded. He lifted his mug and seemed irked to discover it empty. "I'm fine," he said curtly.

Jessie should have taken a hint and backed off. But she couldn't, not when he was only a few feet from her, close enough to touch. She wasn't brave enough to reach across the coffee table and give his hand a consoling squeeze. But she was too stubborn to let the conversation die. "Did you find a place to stay last night?"

He flinched, then recovered. "Yes."

"A motel?"

"An apartment."

Now it was her turn to be startled. "An apartment? Are you planning to stay in town a while?"

"Long enough to find my sister," he said, his tone leaving the distinct impression that the subject of his apartment was off-limits.

"Your sister." The room was definitely cooler than it had been a few minutes ago; the opportunity to get personal had passed. Jessie rose, pushed her chair back into place behind her desk and sat there, lifting a pencil and doing her best to project professionalism. "Have you talked to the police yet? I'm sure you must have. Brothers in blue and all that . . ." She was babbling. She was angry. She didn't understand why Clint had closed down on her—and she hated that it mattered so much to her.

Clint twisted on the sofa so he was facing the desk. He tapped his fingertips together and eyed her intently. "I'm not a cop," he announced.

Jessie fiddled nervously with her pencil as she assessed the man on her sofa. She realized that she was no longer angry with him. He'd misrepresented himself to her yesterday, and he'd smothered her attempts at friendly conversation, but he *was* opening up in some odd way. She only wished she could figure out how, or why, or what he was after.

"You're not a cop," she repeated when his silence extended beyond a minute.

"I didn't exactly lie about it. I mean, I used to be a cop. I quit this past summer."

"What happened?"

"I finished law school and got a job in the D.A.'s office."

"You're a lawyer?" An astonished laugh escaped her. He seemed much too rough-hewn, much too taciturn and modest to be a lawyer. Then again, she supposed that lawyers in a New York City district attorney's office would be different from the flamboyant Southern California lawyers she knew, who made millions off the entertainment industry and the sensational tabloid crimes the city seemed to specialize in.

"When I told you I was a cop," he continued, his voice a low, husky rumble once more, "it was because you were accusing me of shopping for a hooker."

"You were staring at the girls," she reminded him.

"I was looking for Diana." He drummed his fingers against his knee, as if trying to burn off energy. "I was on the force long enough to know what the streets are like for kids—and for prostitutes. It's nasty stuff."

"You don't have to tell me," Jessie said, aware that she and Clint had something in common, after all: a comprehension of how dangerous the streets could be. He seemed so negative, though. Jessie derived her greatest joy from finding the positive side of every situation— even if the situation was kids on the streets. If she couldn't find hope in their plight, she wouldn't work so hard to save them. She wouldn't even care.

Maybe she and Clint didn't have much in common, after all. And maybe she ought to stop dwelling on anything but his sister. "So, have you talked to the local police about Diana?"

"They can't do anything." Again he drummed his fingers on his leg, drawing Jessie's attention to the sleek shape of his thigh. "She's eighteen."

"Eighteen?" Jessie scowled. "She's an adult! Why on earth are you scouring the city for her?"

"I'm overprotective," he conceded.

"Indeed you are." Jessie softened the reproach with a smile. She considered overprotective big brothers kind of sweet, even though at age eighteen she'd hated when her big brother had been overprotective with her.

"The thing is," Clint elaborated, "she dropped out of college and ran off with a guy."

"She eloped?"

Clint winced. "God help her if she did. The guy's bad news. He rides a motorcycle and plays heavy-metal music."

"Oh, my." Jessie couldn't prevent a small giggle from escaping her. "A heavy-metal musician. I guess it doesn't get any worse than that."

Clint obviously didn't share her amusement. He gave her an unrelentingly grim stare. "I'm sure you've seen harder cases. I'm sure your fraternity house here is full of them. But Diana is my sister. She's lived a sheltered life, okay? She's smart and talented and much too pretty for her own good. She got a scholarship to Sarah Lawrence College. We're talking quality here."

"Of course." Jessie considered his doting awfully appealing. Behind his tough-guy demeanor, Clint McCreary was a softy; she liked that.

"Diana went to parochial school. She was taught by nuns. She studied the flute. This is not a savvy girl we're talking about. It's a naive kid who went off to college and it was the first time she was ever on her own. She went to a club near the campus one night and fell in love with the lead singer of the grunge band."

Jessie gave a sober nod. She suspected that if she laughed again, or even smiled the wrong way, Clint would stalk out of her office and never return.

"The musician's name is Mace Bronson."

"Mason?" Jessie wasn't sure she'd heard correctly.

"M-A-C-E, Mace. Like the poison you spray in a mugger's face to keep him from attacking you."

"Mace. Got it." She wrote "Mace Bronson" on a clean sheet of paper, and next to it "Diana McCreary."

Clint seemed to unwind. Evidently, Jessie's jotting notes proved to him that she was taking him seriously. "Mace figured he was better than the rest of the guys in the band, and he was going to make it on his own. He asked Diana to come with him. He told her she was his muse."

"That's a tough line for a girl to resist," Jessie observed.

"Are you speaking from experience?"

Jessie lowered her pencil and glanced up. Was he asking her whether she'd fallen for lines in the past? Or would fall for lines in the future? Did he take a personal interest in her, after all?

Was she ever going to convince herself it didn't matter?

"I work with lots of girls who've fallen for lots of lines," she informed him. "Being the inspiration for a man is one of their favorite fantasies."

Clint scrutinized her thoughtfully. She returned his steady gaze. The light in her office was more revealing than yesterday's glaring sunlight, and she could see him clearly—the shock of thick black hair in desperate need of barbering, the crow's-feet accenting his deep-set eyes, the worry tugging at the corners of his mouth. He was truly, astonishingly gorgeous. Not movie star handsome, not cute like the Beach Boys frozen in 1965 on the poster behind her; Clint possessed the mesmerizing strength of a man who wore his life in the harsh lines and rugged angles of his face, who wasn't afraid to let time and its lessons leave their marks on him.

It was a face Jessie could stare at for a long, long time.

She didn't have a long, long time, however. Clint wanted his sister back, and if Jessie wouldn't help him, he'd go find someone else who would. "Do you know anything about Mace Bronson, besides his name?"

"He's tattooed."

If Clint's tone was anything to go by, he considered tattoos right up there with homicidal tendencies as a sign of bad character. "Are his tattoos visible? If I asked my sources whether they knew this guy, could they identify him by his tattoos?"

Clint shook his head. "It's a saber and a few drops of blood, on his upper left arm. Nothing original. The guy's a cliché. He's a lousy musician, too."

"You've heard him play?"

"Yeah. I went up to visit Diana at her school. She told me she was madly in love with this clown, so I figured I ought to check him out. I drove up to see her, and I met him. The guy was scum."

"Other than being her big brother, what makes you feel you can pass judgment on your sister's boyfriend?" Jessie asked as tactfully as possible.

He must have caught the unspoken criticism in her words. "I was a cop for eight years," he told her. "I dealt with punks on a daily basis. I know scum when I see it. The guy couldn't put together a coherent sentence. He drank too much. He picked fights."

"You saw all that in one day?"

"I saw all that in one hour. He got into a fistfight with a guy who parked too close to his motorcycle. He started tossing back Wild Turkey at one in the afternoon. Okay? He was a piece of dirt."

"Did you point out his flaws to your sister?" If he had, that might have been enough to trigger her decision to run away with the man.

Clint shook his head. "I'm not an idiot. I kept my mouth shut. I didn't want to make her choose sides. The only thing I did was tell her not to let him drive her back to campus on his Harley after he'd chugged down his third bourbon."

"What I'm trying to get at," Jessie probed gently, "is whether Diana ran away not because she was in love with this fellow but because she was ticked off at you."

"No. She wasn't ticked off. She thought I'd like him, and I didn't tell her otherwise."

"When did she come to Los Angeles?"

"She left school a couple of weeks ago. There was nothing secret about it. She called her mother and said she and Mace had decided to head west together so he could cut a record. She said she'd stay in touch, and she has, sort of. She called home twice, but she refused to give my parents an address or a phone number where she could be reached."

"Even if you track her down," Jessie warned, "she may not go back home with you. And if she chooses not to, there's nothing you can do about it. She's legally an adult."

"I know that," he snapped, then raked his fingers impatiently through his hair. "If I could see her for myself, and make sure she's all right, that would be one thing. But I know her. I know she's got stars in her eyes. This guy can't support her. He can't take care of her, and she can't take care of herself. The whole thing's got disaster written all over it."

Jessie mulled over her options. Los Angeles was full of youngsters who needed her more than Clint did, youngsters in far greater danger than Clint's wayward sister.

If Jessie didn't help him, though, not only would he walk out of her life, but he might go chasing through the city until he found his sister, and then he might light into her tattooed boyfriend, and that would only make her cling more tenaciously to Mace Bronson.

"I'll tell you what," Jessie said, selecting her words with care. "I know some people in the music business. I can ask around. Maybe Bronson has been sniffing at their doors, looking for work."

Clint's eyes brightened. "Would you do that?"

"Sure. I've got an appointment to go begging for dollars at MTV next week. Maybe I can push things up with them. And I know someone at Asylum, and someone at Sony—"

"How do you know all these people?"

She chuckled. "Half my life is spent hitting up big shots for donations. If I told you some of the people I've wrung money out of, you'd be impressed."

"I already am impressed."

"But I'm warning you," she added sternly, "if we find your sister and she wants to stay in L.A., you can't do something stupid like kidnap her and bring her home. Legally, she's old enough to move across the country with a man, even if he's got tattoos and his name is Mace. You can't force her to go back to college if she doesn't want to."

"I'm a lawyer," he reminded her dryly. "And a former cop. I know what I can and can't do."

"I'm just saying, if you want my help, you've got to behave yourself." Jessie tempered her lecture with a smile.

Clint wrestled with an answering smile and lost. His lips curved upward into a genuine grin, one that spoke of more than relief. It expressed gratitude, understanding... trust.

Jessie sensed that Clint wasn't the sort of man who gave himself over to trust easily. She thought about her usual victories—getting a kid to talk to his parents, finding a stable foster home for a runaway, saving a child from the big, bad world. Winning Clint McCreary's smile and his trust was a triumph just as rewarding.

It shouldn't matter to her. *He* shouldn't matter to her. But he did.

4

HE HAD TO GET HIS ACT together before he saw Jessie again.

Last night he'd been tormented by strange dreams. In the light of morning, he realized that the dreams hadn't been about his AWOL sister, and they hadn't even been about the ghost, although the mirror had featured prominently in them.

So had Jessie Gale.

In his dreams she'd been the woman in the glass, standing beside him, their reflections moving together, blurring and merging in an erotic dance. He'd pictured her with the mist swirling around her, around him. In his dreams, she had stepped out of the mirror and into his arms, into his bed.

He'd awakened feeling like the randy adolescent he'd once been, the hormone-stricken kid who used to fantasize about golden girls from California materializing in his bed. Cripes. He was a thirty-year-old man, and Jessie Gale was a professional woman, and he had to get a grip.

The dreams, the uneasiness, the shock of seeing a ghost he didn't believe in—all of it eroded his composure, making him behave coldly toward Jessie, almost rudely. He was overloaded, unable to deal with so much stuff and exude charm at the same time. Thank God Jessie didn't seem to hold his lack of manners against him.

A few phone calls on her part uncovered a record producer who claimed he might have met Mace Bronson. The record producer suggested that Jessie and Clint stop by in the late afternoon. Clint promised to return to Rainbow House to pick her up at four o'clock, and then made a quick exit. If he'd stuck around another minute, he was afraid he might start describing his dreams to her—or worse, trying to make them come true.

Steering his car away from the curb in front of the shelter, he cruised the streets surrounding the USC campus. He slowed down as a supermarket loomed into view a block ahead. Maybe he would feel more normal if he stocked up on food. If waking up in a haunted apartment with that wretched mirror glowering at him from the wall had been disconcerting, he'd been equally put out by the fact that he'd had to go to a fast-food joint for breakfast because his kitchen cupboards were bare.

He parked near the entrance of the supermarket and went inside. In his Manhattan neighborhood, real estate was a rare commodity; the food stores were compact, their narrow aisles crammed with teetering towers of merchandise. This vast, airy Los Angeles store appealed to him.

The produce section had all sorts of exotic items on display: kiwis, pineapples, a dozen varieties of mushrooms and more brands of tofu than any sane consumer could possibly wish for. Shaking his head in amazement, he wheeled his grocery cart past the fruits and vegetables in search of Northeastern winter basics: coffee, orange juice, cereal.

The cylindrical cartons of oatmeal in the cereal aisle caught his attention. They reminded him of the two wiseass boys in the kitchen at Rainbow House, one of them—Victor, was it?—mouthing off at Jessie and Jessie returning his salvos, quip for quip. For all her alluring Southern California beauty, the woman was tough. She knew how to handle punks.

She also knew how to navigate through the mine field of brother-sister relationships.

Maybe she was right. Maybe Clint was being overly protective of Diana. But Jessie didn't know how helpless Diana was, how much she relied on being able to giggle and flirt her way out of any predicament—and how lousy the odds were that the predicament she was in right now was something she could giggle and flirt her way out of. Diana's mother pampered her, and her father—Clint's father—viewed her as a gift from heaven, as precious as fine crystal. They treated her with a delicacy that didn't teach her much in the way of survival instincts or common sense.

Clint had been twelve when Diana was born. He'd been a surly, angry child, and he hadn't exactly warmed up to his stepmother. But then suddenly there was this infant in the house, a princess, a jewel, a new life to fill the gaping hole left by the death of Clint's mother. As much as he'd wanted to hate his baby sister, Clint had wound up spoiling her, too.

And now this. An obnoxious metal-head had whisked her off to Southern California, where she was going to wind up totally dependent on him or, even worse, on the streets. Diana had never held down a job in her life. But she was too headstrong and proud to cry to her parents for the money to come home. If things didn't work out with Mace Bronson—and Clint would bet the contents of his savings account they wouldn't—Diana would panic. Ill-equipped to support herself, she would do something drastic.

Like wind up on a street corner, where if she was lucky, a good-hearted soul like Jessie—or a defiantly overprotective big brother like Clint—would find her before someone else did.

He tossed a box of cornflakes into his cart, then headed to the next aisle for coffee, then back to the produce section for a bunch of bananas, which were priced a hell of a lot cheaper than Clint would have paid in New York. He added a few bags of chips to the cart, a bottle of orange juice, a quart of milk, a package of Swiss cheese and a loaf of something called Wheat-Berry Seven-Grain bread, which struck him as hilariously Californian. Then he pushed his cart to the front of the store and took his place in one of the checkout lines.

The line moved sluggishly. Clint skimmed the covers of the tabloids racked beside the cashier's counter. A pair of TV stars had swapped spouses. A two-headed goat had been born on a submarine. You could eat nothing but brownies for a week and lose ten pounds, details on page fourteen.

Bored, he glanced at the cashier. She was around Diana's age, with talonlike fingernails painted metallic blue and a gold stud skewering the skin near her left nostril. He shifted his gaze higher, to the broad panes of glass comprising the front wall of the store. Between the banners and posters advertising double coupons and a special sale on cantaloupes, he glimpsed cars driving along the street, and a few pedestrians. A woman dressed all in red walked an Irish setter on a matching red leash. Two preteen boys who reminded Clint of the breakfast cooks at Rainbow House glided by on Rollerblades. A woman with long, black hair and porcelain pale skin strolled slowly down the sidewalk, pausing to gaze at one of the posters or perhaps to check out her reflection in the glass.

The ghost.

Just as when he'd seen her in the mirror in his apartment, Clint found himself unable to move, to speak, to breathe. The woman on the other side of the glass had the same sable hair, the same fragile features, the same enigmatic smile. She was real, though, not shrouded in mist or gowned in a pale satin gown, but dressed in a short-sleeved knit sweater and tailored slacks, with a purse hanging from her shoulder on a strap. When she brushed her hair back from her cheek, Clint glimpsed a thick gold hoop adorning her earlobe.

Apparently done inspecting herself, the woman pivoted and resumed her stroll. A shudder wrenched Clint, and he turned to discover the cashier staring at him in bemusement. "Twenty-three dollars and fifty-four cents," she said, her hand outstretched.

Clint wondered how many times she'd announced the total without his hearing her. He handed her a twenty and a five, grabbed the two paper bags into which she'd loaded his purchases, and raced out the door, ignoring her when she shouted, "Hey, mister, your change!"

Outside the store, he gazed down the sidewalk, searching for the ghost-woman. She must have turned the corner or gotten into a car. If she was anywhere on the street he would have seen her.

He let out a long, shaky breath and slumped against the fender of his car. Bad enough that he'd seen a ghost in that damned mirror in his apartment; far worse that he'd seen the ghost's twin, her clone, her veritable embodiment sauntering down a street a few miles from the mirror. Had he only imagined her? Had he gone stark raving bonkers?

Or had he been hoodwinked, played for a fool in some sort of elaborate setup? Last night he'd wondered whether the mirror was in fact a one-way looking glass, and a real woman had been standing on the other side of it, illuminated just enough to appear as a translucent vision on his side.

Not simply a real woman. *That* real woman, the one he'd just seen walking past the supermarket.

Why would anyone want to con him, though? Why would anyone go to so much effort to drive an ex-cop from New York insane?

He scanned the block one last time and noticed a liquor store across the street. It was much too early for a drink, but he saw the wisdom in stocking up. While a few beers wouldn't clarify anything, they'd make his confusion easier to endure.

His shopping done, he got back into his car. A quick glance into his rearview mirror revealed nothing but the windshield of the car parked behind him. No black-haired, chalky-skinned ghost-woman floated into his range of vision.

It had to be a scam. Everything was too pat, too well organized: the visitor from out of town, the available apartment, the apparition in the mirror. If he hadn't spotted the woman outside the supermarket, he might have believed he'd actually seen a ghost last night.

He couldn't begin to guess what the point of such a stunt might be, or why anyone would choose him as its target. Perhaps the whole thing was simply a practical joke, and he was going to wind up on some "Candid Camera" home video type show.

In any case, he was going to keep an eye on his back and a hand on his wallet.

He navigated his way to Wilshire Boulevard without getting lost. Two full days in the city, and he hardly even noticed the palm trees anymore, the abundance of summery greenery, the Spanish tile roofs and convertible cars. He tried to revive his memory of the raw, sleety weather he'd left behind in New York, but it seemed less real than the carnal dream he'd had last night, the one featuring Jessie Gale and himself and the mirror.

He parked the car and collected his purchases from the trunk. As he reached the front door, shifting his bags in his arms and digging in his pocket for his key, an attractive blond woman opened the front door from inside, obviously on her way out of the building. "You look like you could use a hand," she said.

He could use a double shot of sanity, but he didn't say that. "Thanks. If you could just hold the door open for me—"

"I can do better than that," she said, relieving him of the bag with the bananas and coffee. Her hair color was a bit too perfect to be real, and the creases framing her mouth were deep enough to place her in the vicinity of middle age. "You're new in Bachelor Arms, aren't you?" she asked.

He wasn't in the mood for small talk, but she was being nice so he had to be nice back. "I've taken an apartment for the month."

"One-G," she guessed, carrying the bag directly to his apartment once he and his remaining parcels had made it inside the front door. "I heard someone had picked up the lease. You must be a brave soul. The last person who rented that apartment—"

"Ran away screaming in the night," Clint finished her sentence. "I know."

"You don't look like the type to run away." She waited until he'd unlocked his apartment door, then shifted the sack of groceries to her left arm and extended her right hand to him. "I'm Jill Foyle."

"Clint McCreary," he said, setting a bag down on the floor so he could shake hands with her.

"Welcome to Bachelor Arms." Her smile was bright, her teeth as white as the chic tennis outfit she wore. "Don't worry about that ghost, now. The worst she can do to you is make your biggest fear come true."

"If that's the worst, it sounds pretty bad," he remarked, taking the last bag of groceries from her. "But it doesn't matter. I don't believe in ghosts." He almost added that he had a damned good reason not to believe in this particular ghost, having just seen her strolling down a street near USC. But he had too much on his mind to get into a long discussion about an allegedly supernatural con job with his new neighbor.

Her smile widened. "You saw the plaque outside the front door, didn't you? *Believe the legend*," she intoned mysteriously. Then she laughed and backed away. "I've got to run, but I live in 2-B if you need anything. This is a very friendly building. Give a holler if that old ghost gives you any trouble." With a farewell wave, she pivoted and headed out the front door.

It didn't take Clint long to put away the groceries. He glanced at the kitchen clock. Not quite eleven. He had hours to kill before he could be with Jessie again.

Correction: he had hours to spend combing the city for his sister on his own before he and Jessie would meet with her friend, the record company executive. That was what his time in Los Angeles was supposed to be about: tracking Diana down. It had nothing to do with Jessie.

Yet when he emerged from the kitchen and his vision filled with the sight of that grotesque mirror...

Whoever the hell the ghost was, whatever the hell her game was, Clint didn't care. What he cared about was that he'd spent last night dreaming about a woman he hardly knew, and dreaming about her in the most erotic terms. If the ghost in the mirror didn't make him crazy, his adolescent crush on Jessie would.

He had to get away from the mirror, and away from his own stupid fantasies. Scooping up his keys, he stormed out of the apartment and back outside to the car. There were a zillion neighborhoods for him to explore, a zillion people to question. He didn't need Jessie.

THE TWO GUYS SET UP IN Lafayette Park could have been runaways like all the others he'd seen, except that they were equipped with a portable amplifier, a guitar, a bass and a mike. They could have been any up-and-coming rock combo, except that they stank.

Clint leaned against a lamppost, trying not to grimace as they butchered an old Jimi Hendrix song. The minute the massacre was over, Clint pulled a dollar bill out of his pocket and dropped it into the bowl the performers had set on the amp. It was just like regular cop work, Clint thought with a wry smile—you pay your sources to talk, and you hope you get your money's worth.

"You guys wouldn't by any chance know a fellow named Mace Bronson, would you?"

The two musicians looked at each other blankly. They couldn't have been much past their late teens, and Clint wondered where they'd come up with the money for their instruments. The bowl had only a few singles and some coins in it.

Maybe they'd stolen the instruments. If they'd stolen them from Mace, they would have done the world a kindness.

"Is he, like, a supplier?" the thin, ponytailed bass player asked.

Clint studied the kid's face. His expression wasn't just blank; it was erased, bleached out. Negated. "Supplier of what?" he asked casually.

"Hey, man." The guitarist had a buzz cut and his arms were covered in tattoos. "Fer-get it, man." He sounded as if he had cotton wads stuffed under his tongue.

"Supplier of what?" Clint persisted. He wasn't a policeman anymore, and even if he were, this wasn't his precinct. But when he saw young kids as stoned as these two were, he wanted to knock their heads together to snap them out of their trances. And he wanted to knock their supplier's head right through a concrete wall.

"Hey, man. It's nothin'. We don't know no supplier," the guitarist said.

In their current state, they probably didn't know much of anything. But Clint kept his irritation under wraps. Who knew what state Mace Bronson was in right now? Or—God forbid—Diana? "Mace Bronson's a musician, just starting out like you. Any chance your paths might have crossed?"

"Never heard of the dude," said the guitarist, who seemed marginally more lucid than the bassist.

"He's traveling with a lady named Diana." Clint produced Diana's photo from a pocket in his blazer and showed it to the two. "Have you ever seen her?"

"Oh, man, she's pretty," the bassist said.

The guitarist took the photo and stared long and hard at it. "I seen her."

"You have?"

"At a club, I think. Everybody hangs out there."

"I don't remember her," the bassist argued.

"You don't remember nothin'," his partner snapped. "Yeah, she was passing through. I remember her right by the edge of the stage, where all the groupies hang. You know, open mike, she came with someone and maybe she left with someone else. She was that kind of chick."

She wasn't that kind of chick at all. At least, she hadn't been when she'd left home for Sarah Lawrence. "She left with someone else?"

"Maybe I'm wrong there." The guitarist handed the photo back to Clint. "I think it was her I saw."

"What club?"

"Who the hell knows? Listen, she was with a musician, so I didn't go near her, you know? A man's gotta have some honor."

"This Mace guy," the bassist said, "is he a supplier?"

Clint sighed and tucked the photograph back into his blazer pocket. "Listen, you two—do yourselves a favor and dry out. It'll improve your performance." *Anything* would improve their performance.

He slipped another dollar into their bowl before he left, knowing it would likely be applied toward the purchase of some illegal substance but feeling grateful for the glimmer of information they'd provided. Diana might have been seen at a club, with a musician. She might have left with someone else. She might be hanging with the groupies.

Clint wanted to strangle her for being such an idiot. He was grinning as he left the street musicians, though, and there was a spring in his step. She was around somewhere, with Mace or with someone like him, wasting time and associating with creeps—but she was alive, off the streets. That alone was cause for celebration.

If only he had someone to celebrate with.

Near where he'd parked his car he spotted a phone booth. In this day of cellular phones, he wasn't surprised to find it empty. He could only hope it worked.

In the same pocket where he kept Diana's picture, he had stashed Jessie's card. She was undoubtedly busy. She'd reserved four o'clock for Clint, but he had no claim on the rest of her day.

Yet she was enough of a bleeding heart that he could convince himself she'd be glad to hear he'd found someone who might have seen his sister. Sliding a quarter into the slot, he dialed the number on the card.

"Rainbow House," someone answered.

"Jessie Gale, please."

"Who's calling?"

"Clint McCreary."

He heard a click as he was put on hold, and then Jessie's voice, slightly bemused. "Clint?"

She probably thought he was a pest. He'd interrupted an important meeting, a vital counseling session with a runaway who was going to clam up and disappear from Rainbow House because Clint had dragged Jessie away when she'd been on the verge of a breakthrough, and Jessie would never forgive Clint for having cost her one of her precious kids.

"I'm sorry. I shouldn't have bothered you—"

"I'm not bothered," she assured him, her voice so warm and inviting he almost believed her. "Are you okay? You sound kind of scratchy."

"I'm calling from a public phone. There's a lot of traffic noise." He closed his eyes so he wouldn't have to stare at the obscene graffiti inked across the Plexiglas walls of the booth. "I met some guys who think they might have seen Diana."

"Really? Oh, Clint, that's wonderful! Where did they see her? Where is she? *How* is she?"

"I don't know. They weren't sure it was really her. Actually, only one of them thought he might have seen her. And he was blitzed out of his mind. They both were." The more he said, the more he realized that if ever a lead had been dead on arrival, this was it. "It probably doesn't mean squat," he concluded.

"Listen to me, Clint. We're going to find your sister. Don't go negative on me."

"Negative's my middle name," he muttered. "I'm sorry I'm bothering you. I should let you get back to work."

"You're not bothering me," she said quickly, as if afraid he was about to hang up. "Tell me what's on your mind."

He faltered. Once, many years ago, his life had spiraled so seriously out of control he thought he would never get over it. He had, though. He'd recovered by learning to protect himself, by promising never to let anything or anyone come too close to him, by conditioning himself to expect the worst. He'd developed scars, and he'd jettisoned the ability to believe in anything beyond what he saw with his own two eyes.

But he'd seen the ghost. And the woman who resembled the ghost, strolling down a street.

And he'd seen Jessie, a woman so kind and honest and trustworthy he couldn't imagine what she'd been doing in his X-rated dream—except for the fact that he *had* imagined it, all too vividly. "Do you really want to know what's on my mind?"

"More than anything," she insisted.

The depth of sincerity in her voice touched him. He opened his eyes and read Blow Jobs, Five Dollars, followed by a phone number, scratched into the metal tray beneath the phone. Wincing, he closed his eyes again. "I had a dream last night," he admitted, too unnerved by the events of the last twenty-four hours to come up with a plausible lie.

"Oh? What about?"

You. You and me making love. "What it's about doesn't matter. The thing is, I don't dream."

"Everyone dreams, Clint. Sometimes people don't remember their dreams in the morning, but everybody has dreams."

"I don't."

She let out a gentle, sympathetic laugh. "Obviously, you do. Los Angeles is a city full of dreams. I'm not surprised one found you."

Geez. She was at her office. He had things to do, too. Why were they wasting time discussing his dream?

Because he couldn't bear to sever his connection to her, that was why. He couldn't bear to hang up. "You make it sound like dreams are just floating around the ozone, looking for a brain to invade."

Amusement colored her tone when she demanded, "Tell me about this dream of yours. Was it upsetting?"

"No."

"Is something else bothering you? Your sister? I know we're going to find her, Clint. You said you met—"

"Those kids didn't know what they were talking about," he said. "They were zonked."

"Even so, they might have seen her. Why not assume they did? It's no crime to be optimistic."

"It makes no sense to be optimistic if you have no grounds for it."

"It's as logical to anticipate the best as to anticipate the worst. If I were a pessimist, I wouldn't be doing social work. I'd find another job."

"Right. Like police work."

"Or law. Lawyers tend to be negative."

"We're negative because so many good cases get thrown out on technicalities. Or because we convict a creep but the jails are too crowded to hold him, so he gets to walk. A few years on a police beat—or a few months in the D.A.'s office—and you learn not to anticipate the best."

"I'll tell you what, Clint—you can be as pessimistic as you want, and I'll be as optimistic as I want. I'll be yin to your yang."

To his surprise, Clint smiled. The idea of being yin and yang with Jessie appealed to him, especially when he pictured the two shapes fitting together, curling into each other like two bodies locked in a sexual embrace. He shouldn't have thought about it in public, though. His jeans suddenly felt a little snug.

"I won't take any more of your time, Jessie," he said to avoid telling her the truth: that thinking about her had an uncomfortable effect on his anatomy. "I know you've got things to do. So do I."

"Then you do your things and I'll do mine. And at four o'clock we'll join forces and do things together."

"Right. I'll see you then."

He did have things to do: more circuits to drive through the city, more shop clerks and pedestrians and drug-dazed street musicians to question. He wanted to scour neighborhoods, talk to people, check in with the local police department. He wanted to find his sister.

But for a brief moment he could stand in the battle-scarred enclosure of a phone booth and think about Jessie: the optimistic social worker, the sensual star of his dreams, the only woman he wanted in his mirror. He could think about yin and yang and the way she would fit with him, the way her curves would mold to him and her body would take his.

It wasn't going to happen. He wasn't going to complicate his life with a quickie West Coast fling. But a man could dream—even if he happened to be a man who never dreamed.

Closing his eyes one last time, he let his memory of Jessie Gale's husky, sexy laughter reverberate inside him, in his mind, in his soul, in the place where, last night, a dream had slipped into his consciousness.

5

"YES, I'M AFRAID I've had the misfortune of meeting Mace Bronson," said Gary Balducci.

Jessie and Clint were seated side by side in Gary's corner office overlooking Santa Monica Boulevard. On one beige wall hung what appeared to be an antique tapestry; on another, an array of framed posters promoting the various rock groups whose albums Gary produced. Although Gary was a boyish-looking thirty-two-year-old, he was a major player in the recording industry.

Jessie wasn't daunted by powerful executives. She spent much of her working life hobnobbing with them in her quest for funds for the shelter. In fact, they nearly always welcomed her into their elegant office suites. In Hollywood, the more successful many entertainment VIPs became, the more eager they were to give their money away.

If anything, she found Clint McCreary more intimidating than Gary Balducci and his ilk. Clint's power didn't come from affluence or corporate rank. He was an ex-cop, an assistant D.A., a quiet, stone-hard New Yorker who believed in his goals as much as Jessie believed in hers. His strength came from something inside him, something that darkened his eyes as he appraised the world around him, something that gave his posture an indomitable strength and his movements a purposeful edge.

His power also came from the fact that he was incredibly sexy. When he'd shown up at Rainbow House at precisely four o'clock, he was wearing a fresh oxford shirt that revealed the broad frame of his shoulders without calling attention to them, and the same jeans he'd had on that morning, the softly faded denim hugging his long legs and narrow hips. He had a runner's build, lean and athletic, the kind of physique Jessie had always been partial to.

She had to stop noticing such things about him. She had to stop responding to his unbearably beautiful eyes, and his thin, expressive lips. She had to stop trying to figure out why sadness lurked in his smile and anger smoldered in his gaze—and most important, she had to stop imagining there was anything she could do to assuage that sadness, that anger. Just because she was a social worker didn't mean Clint wanted her social working on him. And just because she was a woman didn't mean Clint wanted to feel her lips against his, her gaze meeting his in passion.

She told herself she'd changed into her floral print skirt—which, thank goodness, she'd left at her office yesterday—only because she was paying a call on Gary Balducci at his corporate headquarters, not because she wanted to look nice for Clint. She told herself, at least a hundred times, that he was from the opposite end of the country, in town for one reason alone, and once his problem with his sister was resolved he would be gone from Jessie's life forever.

But she honestly didn't want to listen to her own warnings.

"So," she said to Gary, "you met the infamous Mace Bronson. When was he here?"

"Let's see, it was less than a week ago. . . ." Gary did a quick mental calculation. "It must have been . . . Friday morning. I remember because I was eating a guacamole bagel—"

"A guacamole bagel?" Clint blurted out, sounding both amused and repulsed. He'd been letting Jessie do all the talking up to now, but obviously the concept of gua- camole bagels was so outrageous he had to speak up.

"That was the Friday take-out special at The Mystic Bagel, and I always order the special. Thursday the spe- cial was the Reuben bagel. Wednesday it was the choc- olate-chip bagel. Friday was definitely the guacamole bagel, and I was eating it when Bronson came in with his demo tape. I listened to it and told him thanks but no, thanks."

Having finally entered the conversation, Clint took over. "What did he do when you turned him down?"

"He flew into a rage."

Jessie could feel Clint's tension as if it were an electri- cal field emanating from him, causing the air around him to vibrate. In her peripheral vision she saw his hand furl into a fist on his knee. "Was he violent?" he asked, his voice low and chilly.

Gary shook his head and grinned. "When you're talk- ing about heavy-metal musicians, violence is relative. He did use some ripe language, I'll tell you that. Things I wouldn't want to repeat in front of Jessie."

Jessie rolled her eyes. "Trust me, Gary—I've heard language that would make even you blush."

"Jessie, darling, I'd love for you to make me blush," Gary teased, then leaned back in his leather chair and regarded the photograph of Diana that Clint had given him. "I wish I could say this was the woman Mace Bronson had with him, but it isn't. The woman with him was a metallina."

"A what?"

"A lady metal-head. She was a female version of Bronson—tattooed, scraggly hair, overdosing on attitude. Your sister—" he handed the photo back to Clint "—looks too sweet to be hanging out with the likes of Mace."

"Did he leave you an address where he could be reached?" Clint asked.

"Over my protests. There was no way I'd ever want to get in touch with him—unless, of course, I discovered my gold pen missing after his departure." Gary shoved several papers around on his desk, lifted his leather blotter, poked through one of the drawers. Clint leaned forward, as if prepared to get a warrant and search the desk himself if Gary didn't produce the address in a matter of minutes. He must have gotten plenty of practice performing searches during his days as a policeman.

She couldn't picture him in a policeman's uniform. She couldn't picture him dressed like a lawyer, either. Jeans suited him perfectly, and his cotton shirts conveyed a mixture of formality and informality, and when he rolled up the sleeves to reveal his sinewy, lightly haired forearms...

Damn it, she really had to stop thinking about him that way.

"Ah, here it is." Gary unearthed a slip of paper from the rubble cluttering his drawer. He squinted at the paper long enough to make sure it contained the information Clint was after. "Yeah, this is it. Your Mr. Bronson is renting a place down in Florence, which—believe me, Clint—doesn't exactly resemble its Italian namesake.

Not what you'd call a pretty neighborhood. I hope your sister knows some Tae Kwon Do."

Clint's tension increased another few degrees. He sat perfectly still, yet Jessie could feel the air crackling around him, his fury practically radioactive.

He scowled at the slip of paper before passing it to Jessie. "Do you know where that address is?"

"I'm familiar with the general area." Her job took her to many of the city's less picturesque neighborhoods. Handing the paper back to Clint, she said, "I'm sure I can find it."

He pushed himself to his feet and extended his right hand to Gary. "Thanks. You may have saved a life."

"Gee, I thought saving lives was Jessie's department." Gary's grin made him look ridiculously young, no older than some of the kids whose lives she supposedly saved. "Glad I could help. Anything Jessie asks of me, I'll do it. Climb mountains, swim oceans, provide addresses." He eyed her wistfully. "Tell me, love, when are you going to run off with me to one of those quickie chapels in Las Vegas?"

She smiled and shook her head. "You know what they say about the ice cube's chances in hell."

Gary groaned. "I don't get it. I'm rich, I'm gorgeous, and you'd never have to pay for another CD. I'd get them all for you for free."

"Gee, now I'm tempted," she teased. "Free CDs . . . I don't know, Gary. I'll give it some thought."

Clint didn't join their laughter, but his frown faded slightly as he gazed first at Gary and then at Jessie. "Thanks again," he said, then gestured for Jessie to precede him out of the office.

In the hall of the high-rise building that housed the record company's corporate offices, he lapsed into a speculative silence, his strides measured, his thumb sliding along the crease where the paper with Mace Bronson's address was folded. Jessie wanted to ask him how he planned to continue his search. But before she could ask him what his next step would be, he spoke. "Is Gary Balducci your boyfriend?"

The question startled her, not just because she'd assumed Clint had been thinking about his sister and Mace Bronson but because she hadn't expected him to take an interest in her social life. "No," she said, wishing she weren't so flattered. "As they say in Hollywood, we're just friends."

"I thought that when they say that in Hollywood, it means the exact opposite."

Jessie grinned. "Well, in this case it's the truth. Gary has a thousand girlfriends. If I were his girlfriend, I'd be number 1,001. He's a much better person to have as a friend."

Clint pressed the elevator button. Jessie wished she had the nerve to ask him whether he'd be better as a lover or a friend. She could guess...but given that she was never going to have him as her lover, she would like to find out what sort of friend he would make.

The elevator arrived. "Maybe it's L.A.," he muttered half to himself as he gestured for Jessie to enter the car ahead of him.

"What's L.A.?"

He followed her in and the doors hummed shut. "The way people relate to each other. There's all this implied..." He drifted off, unable to come up with the right word.

"All this implied *what?*" she asked.

"Intimacy."

Hearing him utter the word had a disturbing effect on her. The hell with what sort of friend he would make. She would much rather think of him in the context of intimacy, *real* intimacy, a lover's intimacy.

And that was dangerous.

"You barely meet somebody," he elaborated, "and the next thing you know, they're confiding in you. You ask a friend for a favor, and all of a sudden he's begging you to run off to Las Vegas and marry him. It's all so . . ." Again he groped for the right word. "I don't know. So personal."

"That's Los Angeles for you," she said with a smile. "People are more open here. They don't try so hard to protect themselves. It's hot, and people don't wear much clothing—and they don't wear much emotional clothing, either." The elevator doors opened onto the ground floor, and she and Clint stepped out into the vaulted lobby. "It's one of the things I like about living here," she went on as they crossed the black marble floor to the main exit. "The openness, the way people don't knock themselves out trying to hide what's going on inside them."

Clint mulled over what she'd said. She wondered if he suspected her of trying to find out what he was hiding. She wouldn't pry—she'd learned from her dealings with teenagers that prying was the worst way in the world to get someone to open up. But she was mighty curious about the secrets lurking in Clint's soul.

"You aren't a California native?" he asked.

"I grew up just outside Philadelphia."

He halted and gaped at her in astonishment. With a short, bemused laugh, he shook his head and resumed his trek across the lobby.

She accelerated her pace to keep up with his lanky gait. "What's so funny about my being from Philadelphia?"

The glass door swung open automatically, and they exited into the warm late afternoon. A fountain outside the building sent a white plume of water upward, and a breeze blew stinging droplets of moisture against her cheeks. Clint didn't even glance at the fountain; he was staring at her again. "You look like such a typical California girl."

"A California girl?" She chuckled. "Just because I've got a Beach Boys poster hanging in my office doesn't mean anything—except that I like the Beach Boys. And don't forget, in that song they did about California girls, they said East Coast girls were hip."

They strolled around the fountain to the sidewalk and down the block to where Clint's car was parked. Jessie had offered to drive, since she knew her way around the city better than he did, but he'd said he didn't like vans. "They remind me of surveillance jobs," he'd explained.

He unlocked the passenger door for her and touched her elbow as she lowered herself into her seat. With an almost shy smile, he straightened up and closed the door behind her, then moved around the car to the driver's side. She wasn't used to chivalry, but Clint had a certain old-fashioned honor about him. It was that quaint, charming honor that compelled him to protect his sister—who probably would be a whole lot happier without his protection.

"So, tell me, Clint—how am I a typical California girl?" Jessie asked once he was settled behind the wheel.

Instead of turning on the engine, he twisted in his seat to look at her. "You're blond and blue-eyed, and . . ." He drifted off, ruminating. His eyes, she realized, held more than anger, much more. She sensed a tenderness in them, a soothing hint of blue blended in with the steel gray, the irises rimmed with a thin black circle. Clint had what she and her girlfriends used to call bedroom eyes.

And that was another dangerous thought.

"You've got more of a suntan than a blond person is supposed to have," he said. "You look . . . I don't know. Healthy."

"I take it people in New York look sickly?"

"As a matter of fact, yeah, they do." He laughed, apparently aware of how absurd that sounded. At last he turned forward and started the engine. "There's no sunshine in New York in November," he explained as he eased the car into the flow of traffic. "If you see someone with a tan, you assume they went to a tanning parlor, or they just got back from Aruba. A winter tan in New York isn't natural."

"It's natural here. Turn right at the corner—we're heading south." She pulled her sunglasses from her purse and slid them on. "So, everyone is pallid and anemic in New York, huh."

"In November, yeah."

"Philadelphia was like that, too." She smiled. "I'd never been to L.A. until I finished graduate school. I decided to treat myself to a two-week vacation before I started my first job. I wanted to do the whole tourist route—houses of the stars, Graumann's Chinese Theater, Disneyland."

"You came and couldn't leave," he guessed.

"Yes, but not because of Disneyland." She smiled at her own predictability. "There were so many kids on the streets, Clint. They really flood the city during the summer. As it turned out, I didn't get to Disneyland until I'd been living here almost a year. By the time my first week of vacation was over, I'd talked my way into a job with the city's social services department. Within a year, I'd put together Rainbow House."

"And then you went to Disneyland."

"With four runaways as my guests."

He shot her a quick look. "What are you, a saint?"

Long after he turned away from her she let her gaze linger on him. She heard criticism in his tone, or at the very least disbelief. "No," she said firmly, "I'm not a saint. The whole thing was selfish, actually. I realized Disneyland would be more fun for me if I didn't have to go alone."

He sent her another brief, skeptical glance and then focused on the road ahead. It occurred to her that he thought she was lying, or overly altruistic. He seemed unable to accept that someone might find a place like Disneyland more enjoyable if she had a few kids to share it with.

"I like children," she added.

"Then how come you aren't married and raising a few of your own?"

"I hope to have children someday," she said, even though her marital status was none of his business. "Right now I'm doing other things. We need 110 South. There's the sign up ahead."

He followed her directions, letting the subject of her personal life drop. They cruised south on the freeway for a few miles, Clint's eyes on the road and Jessie's thoughts on Clint.

She wasn't pleased with the notion that he considered her saintly. Men didn't make passes at saints.

She sternly reminded herself that she didn't want Clint making a pass at her. And far from being a saint, she considered herself one of the most selfish people she knew, if also one of the luckiest. Few people were able to make a career of the work they loved best.

The next several minutes passed in silence. Traffic wasn't too heavy, and Clint left the radio off, leaving Jessie with little to distract her from the man beside her—and from his questions about her single status. She could have been married today, if she'd been willing to accompany Danny to Oregon when he'd decided he'd had enough of L.A. It wasn't as if she were a spinster, hopeless and doomed to a future without children of her own.

But she didn't want to have a child out of wedlock, and she didn't want to get married until she found someone who shared her outlook on life. Clint McCreary clearly wasn't that someone.

As if there were any reason on earth for her to be contemplating him in connection to marriage.

"This is our exit," she announced.

He veered off the freeway and headed east, driving slowly through the densely settled streets, past grocery stores and low-slung cinder block apartment buildings, past squat bungalows and chain-link fences and walls of graffiti. "Cripes," he muttered. "It looks like the Bronx, only with palm trees."

"I bet the Bronx doesn't have so many red tile roofs," she argued, smiling to prove that even this dismal neighborhood wasn't going to get her spirits down.

His expression remained hard, his mouth set in a grim line. "Give me directions," he said.

His seething anger troubled her. If it picked up steam, he was going to explode the minute he found Bronson—and if he did that, he'd blow his chances with his sister. Jessie had to keep him cool and steady. "Stay on this street a few more blocks," she told him. "When you were a policeman, did you patrol in the Bronx?"

"No."

He glared at a young man loitering on the corner. The kid looked young and cocky, and he wore so many thick gold necklaces they almost looked like chain mail. The punk matched stares with Clint for a moment, then turned away, in some sort of defeat.

"Where did you work?" she asked, struggling valiantly to keep the conversation alive.

"Lower Manhattan."

"Greenwich Village?"

He shook his head. "The Lower East Side. Little Italy, the Bowery."

His laconic tone implied he'd rather not talk about it. As they drove farther into Florence, Jessie realized he was becoming even more tense, gearing himself up for a confrontation with Bronson.

"Clint," she began, then sighed. She didn't have time to ease her way gradually into this. They were only a couple of blocks from the address on the scrap of paper. "Have you figured out what you're going to say when you see him?"

"I'm going to say, 'Give me my sister and I'm out of here.' All I want is Diana."

"She's not an object, Clint. It's not up to Mace to *give* her to you."

"Thanks for the input," he snapped.

"I mean it, Clint. I know you didn't ask me for any advice—turn left at the end of the block, I think that's the street we're looking for." She waited until Clint turned the corner, then continued. "You don't want my advice, but I'd hate to see everything backfire. You can't haul Diana off like she's a piece of property. You've got to *persuade* her to come with you."

"Yeah, sure. Next thing, you're going to tell me I don't understand women."

"I'll tell you you don't understand teenage girls."

"When I was a cop, I dealt with plenty of teenage girls."

"And they were all hookers, right?" Jessie remembered the way he'd viewed the three runaways she'd rescued near the Civic Center yesterday morning. "This is your sister, Clint. It's a whole different situation. I've worked with dysfunctional families—"

"I don't have a dysfunctional family," Clint cut her off, enunciating the words with obvious loathing. "As a matter of fact, I don't believe in dysfunctional families. There are abusive families, there are poor families, there are crime families, and there are other families. My family is an average working-class family with a spoiled girl who went on a toot without considering the consequences. Okay?"

Jessie scrutinized him. Why had her comment ignited such a defensive response? What was he hiding from her? Perhaps his family was average—but most average families didn't include teenage girls who ran away from elite colleges with their derelict boyfriends and settled in one of the slummier sections of L.A.

"Clint ..."

"Don't diagnose me, all right?" he retorted, his voice rasping with contained fury. "I'm here to get my sister. That's all there is to it. Is that the building we're looking for?" Clint motioned with his head toward a gloomy three-story building of gray stucco a short distance ahead.

Jessie had the wisdom to back down. "That's it," she said, recognizing the number painted on the glass front door.

He cut the wheel sharply and snagged a parking space not far from the building. She didn't wait for him to open her door for her. She had the feeling that, given a choice, he would leave her in the car and enter the building alone. It was a choice she wasn't going to give him.

She was already at the building's front door by the time he'd locked up the car. He glared at her, a warning embedded in his frown. She chose to ignore it; she wasn't going to let him shut her out. She wanted to save his sister almost as much as he did—although she couldn't shake the feeling that this outing had something to do with saving Clint.

They entered the building's dimly lit foyer and studied the row of intercom buttons on a wall panel. None of the buttons was labeled; she and Clint had no way of knowing which one connected with Mace Bronson's apartment.

Not that that was going to stop them. The latch on the inner door was broken, leaving it permanently unlocked. Jessie waited for Clint to comment on the building's shabby condition.

Whatever he was thinking, he held his words. She wished he would let some of his anger out before the pressure got too great. But venting wasn't Clint's style.

Inside the inner door, Clint moved directly to the first apartment he saw and knocked on the door. After a minute, it was opened by a slim young girl no more than seven years old, her hair braided into a remarkable array of bead-bedecked loops and twirls. "Hi," Clint said in an unexpectedly gentle voice. "I'm looking for a man named Mace Bronson."

The girl's eyes were huge. She gazed up at Clint, curious but mute.

Clint tried again. "He's a big white dude, in his early twenties, with dirty blond hair that comes down past his shoulders. He plays guitar. He never smiles—"

"I know him," the little girl volunteered. "He lives upstairs."

"Which apartment?"

"Right above us. We hear that guitar all the time. He plays awful."

"That's the guy. Thanks." Clint started toward the stairs, then stopped and returned to the girl. "Listen, honey, you shouldn't open your door so wide when you don't know the person on the other side. Are you tall enough to see through that hole there?" He pointed to the peephole in the door.

She shook her head solemnly.

"Then use that safety chain," he instructed her, pointing out the chain that hung idly against the doorframe. "Don't open the door so a stranger can get inside. Will you promise me that?"

"Okay."

"Promise," he repeated.

"Okay. I promise."

"Thanks." The smile he gave the little girl caused Jessie's breath to catch. It was so tender, so sweet with concern she wanted to weep. For all his gruffness, his pent-up fury, his overprotectiveness, Clint was in his own way as compassionate as Jessie. He cared about all little girls, not just his sister. He wanted to rescue Diana, he probably wanted to deck Mace Bronson—but first he wanted to make sure a child he would never see again was safe.

The girl continued to watch them until they'd reached the stairs, then closed the door. A faint smile flickered across Clint's mouth when he heard the bolt slide into place, and then his expression reverted to cold determination.

Jessie swallowed the lump of sentiment in her throat and followed him up the stairs.

Reaching the second floor, Clint moved unerringly down the hall to the apartment directly above the little girl's. Jessie remained a couple of steps behind him, willing despite her apprehension to let him fight the first round himself. He banged on the door, and she noticed that his hand was once again knotted into a fist, his knuckles white with tension.

Through the door she heard the muffled sound of loud, sour music. When the door opened, the sound was no longer muffled. A gravelly voice howled through a speaker deep in the apartment, wailing about women's body parts in graphic, insulting language.

The man who filled the open doorway had to be Mace Bronson. Jessie knew this not only from his long, dirty blond hair but from the trite tattoo on his upper arm, visible because he wore no shirt under his leather vest. The smell of cigarette smoke clung to him like bad karma. He held an open bottle of bourbon in one hand.

His sleepy eyes came into focus on Clint, and he sneered. "Well, well, well," he growled. "If it isn't the lawman. How's it going, bro'? Fancy meeting you here."

Clint's fist flexed at his side, but his voice emerged low and steady. "Where's my sister?"

"Diana? The bitch of my life?"

Jessie bit her lip to keep from interfering. She could tell from Clint's posture, from the jut of his chin and the ice in his gaze, that he was barely inches from smacking Bronson right in the center of his smug, nasty grin. "Where is she?" he asked, his voice lower, tighter.

"Damned if I know." Bronson shrugged, causing his vest to rise and fall above his extravagantly muscled chest.

"Give me your best guess." Clint's voice was so taut it cut through the air like a stiletto.

Evidently, Bronson felt its sharpness and straightened up. "She left me, all right? I ain't happy about it. The bitch walked."

"Where did she go?"

"Ran off with another guy."

"What other guy?"

"Beats me."

Jessie imagined Clint would love nothing more than to beat him. Exercising enormous self-control, however, he only repeated the question. "What other guy?"

"He's a musician, I think. He showed his face at a club, and she left with him. I swear, Big Brother, I don't know dip about him. Except he goes by the name Jocko, something like that."

"Where is he? Where does he live?"

The softer Clint's voice became, the more nervous Bronson appeared. "I don't know, man, okay?" he said, sounding both impatient and pleading. "I don't know. He's rich, though. He's got bucks. That's where your wonderful little sister's head is at, okay, buddy? She ran off with a rich mother. It wasn't my choice, okay?"

Clint let out an ominously controlled breath. "Jocko," he said. "He plays in the clubs?"

"I don't know if he plays. He hangs out at the clubs, though—that's the buzz, anyway. Listen, man, I'm sorry, okay? I shoulda told her to stay at Sarah Lawrence and become a nice little sorority girl or whatever, I don't know, get straight *A*s or something. I'm sorry."

"I'll bet you are." His hand still furled into a fist, Clint abruptly spun away and stalked to the stairs, leaving Jessie to offer Bronson a feeble farewell smile before she chased Clint down to the first floor and out of the building.

Blinking in the still-bright afternoon after the murkiness of the tenement, Jessie followed Clint to the car. He said nothing as he unlocked her door; he skipped his usual chivalry and let her open the door and get in without assistance. She watched him through the windshield as he moved around the front of the car to the driver's side. His jaw was still set, pugnaciously angled. His posture was still rigid. He was a man who obviously did battle with his temper on a regular basis, and while he was winning the battle right now, she wasn't sure how long he could hold out before his temper got the better of him.

She wasn't sure why he was even fighting himself. It would be healthier to let all the anger out. His only show of emotion, though, was to slam his door once he was seated behind the wheel.

The air inside the car was hot and stagnant. She wished he would turn on the engine so they could open the automatic windows. But although he inserted the key in the ignition, he didn't twist it. He simply stared at the flat, drab neighborhood surrounding them.

"You're not thinking of going to the clubs," she murmured when his silence lasted long enough to unnerve her.

He tossed her a quick, sharp look. "Why am I not thinking of that?"

"Because it's only five-thirty. None of them will have anything going on right now."

He nodded. Evidently he'd expected her to lecture him on being rational and calming down. Her answer was more practical, and he seemed to appreciate that. "Do you know anything about the city's rock clubs?" he asked.

"A little. I'm sure there are a thousand clubs I've never even heard of, but I've been to a few, and I know about a few more."

He nodded again. "But they don't come alive until late."

"No."

He turned forward again, immersed in thought. "Maybe before I drop you off, you could give me some names of clubs to check out."

In other words, he didn't want her tagging along anymore. Even after her exemplary restraint at Bronson's apartment, he didn't want her with him. He'd spent time in her company that morning, and more time that afternoon, and he'd had all he could take of her.

Oh, for God's sake! What egotism gave her the right to translate his every statement into terms that revolved around her? If he didn't want her to visit the clubs with him, fine. If he wanted nothing but names, fine. Just because every time she looked at him her mind filled with steamy notions didn't mean he was under any obligation to drag her with him everywhere he went.

On the other hand, she really didn't want him to bungle things with his sister. Just because he had refrained from popping Mace Bronson in the nose didn't mean his supply of willpower was going to last through an encounter with Jocko, too. If he didn't handle Jocko properly, he'd risk losing Diana.

What he needed was a chance to replenish his reserves of willpower. A chance to cool down, cool off, and restore his equilibrium before the bell rang for round two.

She waited until he started the engine, then said, "Let's take a different route back. The freeway is going to be a rush-hour nightmare. Hang a left at the corner."

He looked dubious, as if he suspected her of ulterior motives. Well, she'd never taken him for a fool. She *did* have ulterior motives. But he needed to unwind, and to spend a few minutes not obsessing on his sister's troubling attraction to male rockers with names like Mace and Jocko.

It wasn't that Jessie didn't want to say goodbye to him. She was only thinking of his emotional well-being.

Sure. And Mace Bronson was the next Elvis.

So Jessie was selfish. So she wanted to spend a few more minutes with Clint. No big deal. "See that sign?" she said, pointing. "Route 42. That's what we want."

He could have questioned her, or demanded to know exactly where she was navigating him. But although his skepticism remained, turning his eyes a gunmetal gray and denying his mouth a smile, he followed her directions and steered toward Route 42.

Jessie reminded herself of how much more there was to Clint besides anger and brotherly concern. She recalled the way he'd behaved with the little girl in the first-floor apartment. Clint McCreary must have been a good cop. He was certainly a good man.

And regardless of how selfish her motivations were, he deserved the detour she had in mind for him.

6

"THE BEACH? What are you, nuts?"

She answered with a benign smile. "You're in L.A., Clint. When in L.A., do as the Angelenos do."

He drew in a long breath and prayed for serenity. It was one thing not to blow his stack with Mace Bronson, when one wrong move might have meant never finding his sister. But to blow his stack with Jessie would risk losing her respect, her admiration, her willingness to put up with him for a few days.

He tried to tell himself he didn't need her respect and admiration and the rest of it. Finding Diana was the only thing he ought to be worrying about. Finding Diana, finding some clown named *Jocko*—couldn't his sister hook up with a guy with a normal name? he wondered irritably—finding the right rock clubs in Los Angeles ...

He had plenty enough to keep him occupied. He didn't need Jessie Gale.

But he had her company, and he wanted to keep it for as along as he could. He was miles from home, no longer a cop and barely a lawyer, searching an unknown city with nothing but his wits to guide him. And from the moment he'd seen Jessie, he'd been a sucker for her blond hair and her blue eyes and her irresistibly sunny disposition. He'd trusted her, accepted her help and let her navigate him through the unfamiliar terrain of Greater Los Angeles. Because she'd gotten him to Mace Bron-

son's address, he had blindly obeyed her directions out
of Florence. He'd driven west, then northwest, then west
some more, through towns and neighborhoods he didn't
recognize, until all of a sudden they were at Santa Monica State Beach. At sunset. In November, on the cusp of
winter.

"We'll just take a little walk," she urged him, swinging
out of the car before he could stop her. She glanced over
her shoulder and sent him an alluring smile, alive with
dimples and pearly teeth. "There's nothing you can do
to find your sister right now. Besides, how can you travel
all the way to California and never see the Pacific Ocean
up close? Come on, Clint—just a quick walk on the
beach. It'll do you some good."

"I don't take walks on the beach in November," he
muttered, although with the early-evening temperature
hovering around seventy degrees, he couldn't exactly
complain that it was too cold for a seaside stroll. Nor
could he complain that he had no time. At the moment,
with his sister in some jerk named Jocko's clutches and
the rock clubs not yet open for business, time was all he
had.

Sighing, he got out of the car and locked it. The air
held the damp, voluptuous fragrance of the ocean, a
bracing change after the acrid hot-asphalt stench of
Florence. The sand stretched pale and shimmering from
the palm trees bordering the parking lot to the froth-
trimmed edge of the ocean; countless footprints indi-
cated that countless people had enjoyed the beach that
day.

Some people were still enjoying it. Two young men in
swim trunks hit a volleyball back and forth without
benefit of a net. A dapper elderly man wearing a straw
hat and white linen shorts paced the sand with a metal

detector. Two thirty-something women were packing up beach toys and blankets while a half-dozen kids squabbled and whined around them. A gaggle of young ladies near the lifeguard station were removing their office apparel, stripping off layers of nylons and demure blouses and skirts to reveal skimpy bikinis underneath.

"See?" Jessie said, tracing Clint's gaze from one group of sun worshipers to another. "People do come to the beach in November. We've got endless summer here."

"It can't stay this warm all year," he objected. Los Angeles was too far north of the equator to qualify as the tropics.

"It does. I hate to break the news to you, Clint, but there are places in this world that are a lot nicer than New York."

"I'm not sure L.A. is nicer than New York," he argued. Which wasn't to say he considered New York particularly nice. He just wasn't sure whether the monotonously mild climate of Southern California was a good or a bad thing. As bitter as New York's winters might be, Clint believed they built character. Or at least that was what he and millions of other Northerners told themselves as they suffered through the sleet storms and blizzards and arctic winds that howled into their world at this time of year and didn't let go until spring.

Jessie led the way through the palm trees to the sand. She lifted one foot, balancing gracefully on the other leg so she could remove her sandal. Then she balanced on the other leg. "Take your shoes off," she instructed him, as if he'd just arrived from another planet and had no idea what a beach was.

He scowled at her but dutifully removed his shoes and socks. He didn't wait for her to coach him through the rolling up of his jeans, but cuffed the hems to just below his knees and stalked onto the sand, refusing to admit that this outing was the least bit enjoyable for him.

But it was. The sand wasn't scorching, the way it was back home in August, when walking on the beach was as painful as dancing on hot coals. This Southern California sand was soothingly warm and pliant, massaging his toes and dusting his insteps. The whispered rhythm of the waves rolling onto the shore was just as soothing. It was hard for a man to stay upset about his hare-brained sister and her god-awful taste in boyfriends when he was standing barefoot on such smooth white sand, being serenaded by the tides and the sea gulls, being caressed by the humid breezes.

Jessie sauntered past him, her skirt swirling about her calves. The shore winds pressed the lightweight cotton against her thighs and her loose cotton blouse against her breasts. Clint resolutely lowered his gaze to her feet, but they, too, were annoyingly feminine, pale and graceful and accented with intriguing anklebones. Plus they were naked.

He gritted his teeth and turned away. The old man in the straw hat trundled past, leading with his metal detector the way a blind person might lead with a white cane. The women who'd transformed from office workers to beach bunnies jogged past him, giggling and chattering until they reached the water. Without hesitation, they splashed in.

He waited for them to scream. Back home, people always howled in agony when they first entered the ocean, because even on the hottest days of the summer the water was freezing. Either these women were cold-blooded or the water here was warm.

Once she'd crossed the line separating the dry sand from the wet, Jessie pivoted and beckoned to him. "Come on," she called, her voice barely carrying above the wind and the surf. "You've got to stick your toes in the Pacific, or it doesn't count."

What doesn't count? he wondered. But logic didn't seem all that important when a woman with sun-streaked hair and azure eyes was waving him toward the water. A woman with a strong, slender body, broad shoulders and healthy curves and . . . *knees.* Incredible knees. When Jessie gathered up her skirt and forged closer to the edge of the water, Clint saw the exquisite ovals of her kneecaps, the dimples at the backs of her knees, the hint of her luscious thighs above and a full view of her tapering bronze calves below.

Hers were the sort of knees that could star in a guy's most vivid wet dreams. Even a guy like Clint, who had never before given a thought to knees.

As if she were a beacon, drawing him closer, he pursued her to the water's edge. A wave lapped his feet, but he didn't flinch. The ocean really was, if not warm, certainly much milder than the Atlantic waters off Long Island back home. He dared another step into the ocean, and the water closed over his insteps. To the west he saw nothing but an unbroken horizon.

Jessie waded into the water beside him and shielded her eyes with her hand. "Now you can honestly say you've been to California," she said. "Now it counts."

"My being here wouldn't have counted, otherwise?"

"No. You've got to stand in the Pacific."

"I guess thanks are in order. It would have been a bummer to travel three thousand miles, find my sister and go home and discover none of it counted."

She grinned at him. "You're welcome."

A wave rolled in, splashing his shins. It was cool and refreshing, not cold. He thought of the beers chilling in his refrigerator and realized that this was better. He'd rather be standing up to his ankles in the Pacific Ocean with Jessie than drinking a brew by himself in his strange apartment at Bachelor Arms.

"You know what your problem is?"

He gazed at her. The wind had made a mess of her hair, and the pink overtones of the setting sun put a blush in her cheeks. She looked so pretty, with her blouse billowing and flattening against her torso and her chin held high, that he could just about forgive her presumptuousness. "No, Jessie, I don't know what my problem is. Why don't you tell me?"

"You're too solemn. You need to stand in the water more often."

"This may come as a shock to you, but Californians didn't invent beaches. I go to the beach all the time in New York."

"Not in November, you don't."

"All right, not in November. But we've got beaches. We've got sand and surf and the whole thing." A blobby strand of seaweed wrapped itself around his foot, and he bent over to untangle it. He freed his foot from the greenish brown plant and started to straighten up—only to get a handful of water in his face.

The hand belonged to Jessie.

Jerking upright, he sputtered and wiped the water from his eyes. Jessie stood laughing. "What the hell was that for?"

"I'm just trying to loosen you up," she said, then succumbed to fresh giggles. Her laughter soared on the breeze as if it had wings.

Actually, a splash of water didn't bother him. He'd like nothing better than to be laughing with a beautiful, spirited blond California girl—even if she was from

Philadelphia, even if she was a woman, not a girl, even if she was a professional do-gooder with an unrealistically optimistic streak.

But he was a man, and a man did what he had to do. Which, in this situation, was retaliate.

She must have seen the change in his expression. Jamming her hand against her mouth in a vain attempt to smother her laughter, she let out a tiny "Uh-oh," rotated, and tried to scamper away.

The water slowed her down. Light graceful steps turned into trudging slogs that created surges and eddies against her shins. It didn't take long for him to catch up to her, clamp his hand over her shoulder, spin her around and hurl a handful of water into her face.

His hand was much bigger than hers, and the amount of water it held not only drenched her face but soaked the front of her hair. Heavy drops cascaded down onto her shoulders and the neckline of her blouse.

She roared with pretended indignation. "Clint, that's not fair! I barely sprinkled you! Look at me! I'm dripping wet!"

"You wanted me to loosen up? That's how I loosen up."

"I'll loosen you up!" She swung her arms down, scooped up a double handful of water, and flung it at him, splattering his shirt. Both her hands couldn't do as much damage to him as one of his did to her.

His laughter seemed to goad her. She bent down to scoop another double handful, and while she was stooped over he wrenched his hand under the water's surface, flipping a fistful of ocean into her face.

She shrieked and charged at him with all the force of a defensive end—a very wet one who weighed no more than a hundred twenty-five pounds or so. Still, it was enough to knock him off-balance. He stumbled backward, searching for a solid footing on the kelp-choked seafloor.

It was useless. He was going down. But damn it, he was going to take her with him.

The water was no more than a foot deep where they fell, but that was deep enough to soak his jeans when he landed on his butt. It was also deep enough to give Jessie a thorough dousing as she tumbled, gasping and shrieking, into his lap.

"Oh, my God!" She sputtered and splashed, grabbing hold of his thighs as she tried to lever herself off him. "Oh, God—I'm drenched!"

"I thought the term was *loosened up*," he murmured, wishing she would remove her hands from his legs . . . wishing she *wouldn't* remove them. Through the clammy dampness of his jeans he felt the strength in her fingers as she gripped, groped, sought something to push off from. Her touch could make a dead man wake up, and Clint was very much alive. His only hope was that, what with the churning seawater and the heavy, damp denim covering the lower half of his body, she wouldn't be able to see the effect her hands were having on him.

Or those sexy knees of hers. One of them was pressing into his shin, and the other rested against his outer thigh so that she was all but straddling his leg.

And then there were her breasts, their lush roundness visible through the clinging wet fabric of her blouse, her nipples hardened into sharp relief from the water and the wind. Her hair curled about her face in dripping tendrils, raining water down her cheeks and throat and leaving a few beads of moisture on her lips.

Her lips. They were less than an inch from his.

Caution was an essential part of Clint's nature. Even in the most profound rage—when he was going toe-to-

toe with an ass like Mace Bronson, for instance—he
knew how to keep a tight grip on his self-control. But put
a woman like Jessie Gale within kissing range, and he
forgot caution, he let control slip away. He reached out
and took what he wanted.

A wave slapped his side as he circled his arms around
her and drew her to himself. Another wave rocked him
as his mouth found hers. She was his dream come to life,
his adolescent fantasies magnified by a million. To kiss
this woman, this goddess—to kiss her while sitting awkwardly in the shallows of the Pacific...

It was better than anything he'd ever dared to imagine. Better than any kiss he'd ever experienced. Jessie
Gale was indeed a wizard, and her kiss was a tornado
that could carry him over the rainbow.

He slid his hands under her arms to her back. Through
her waterlogged blouse he felt her ribs, the delicate ridge
of her spine, her angular shoulder blades. Closing his
eyes, he could visualize how her back would look un-
clothed, all smooth peach-hued skin sculpted by those
bones, dainty yet strong. He didn't like wimpy women,
weak women, women who gasped and feigned helpless-
ness and behaved passively. He didn't like women who
expected the man to do all the kissing.

Jessie wasn't wimpy or weak. She gave as good as she
got.

Wrapping her arms around him and linking her hands
at the nape of his neck, she returned his kiss with a fearlessness that astonished him. This was a woman who
wasn't afraid of slums, street punks, foul-smelling metal-
heads or record company VIPs—and she wasn't afraid
of kissing a man who made no promises, no declara-
tions, not even the most meaningless sweet talk. Clint

and Jessie had no past, no future, but she seemed willing to accept the present, to make the most of it.

Her lips molded to his, melded with his, opened on a sigh of delight. Her tongue met his and he felt as if a circuit had been completed, sending a current buzzing through his body, lighting him up.

He skimmed his hands down to her hips, cupped the roundness of her bottom and pulled her higher onto him. She moaned, her breath filling his mouth, her lips salty against his tongue. She twirled her fingers through his hair and his hips moved of their own volition, arching against her. With another moan, she tore her mouth from his and nestled her head against his shoulder. Her breath came in ragged gulps. He could scarcely breathe at all.

Somewhere far above him he heard the high-pitched mewing of a gull; somewhere way behind him he heard swimmers romping and laughing. None of it mattered. That he was at a public beach in a state park, that he was sitting in a foot of water, his clothing soggy and the incoming tide lapping at him . . . He didn't care.

All he cared about was the woman in his arms, soft and wet and trembling.

"Are you cold?" he asked, tightening his hold on her and feeling her shiver against him. The sun rode low in the sky, flirting with the horizon.

"No." Her voice came out less than a whisper. Then she gave a small, shy laugh. "Quite the opposite, actually."

Her words caused a spasm of longing to grip him, precisely where she was sitting on him. He shifted under her to alleviate his condition and she gasped as his movements made her aware of that condition. "Oh, Clint . . . You're quite the opposite, too."

"This is a hell of a place to be the opposite."

"Do you want me to get off?"

No. Never. "I suppose you'll have to."

She eased herself out of his arms and off his lap. Her skirt ballooned and then sank in the shallow water, and her cheeks were flushed as she shoved against the weight of her sodden clothes and stood. She extended her hands to him, and he fought the urge to pull her right back into his arms, onto his lap. Instead, he let her haul him to his feet.

As soon as he had his balance she turned away, her cheeks even darker as she pushed her limp, bedraggled hair back from her face. She stared at her skirt, which was flecked with bits of seaweed.

It dawned on him that she was embarrassed. Jessie Gale, who'd kissed him as if kissing were her only purpose in life, as if she were an addict and he was the drug she craved, as if not kissing him would have meant certain death...suddenly wasn't able to look him in the eye.

"Jessie?"

"I'm sorry," she mumbled, splashing through the water to terra firma. "I can't believe . . . God, I can't believe we did that."

He followed her out onto the sand. "It's no big deal." Wrong. It was a very big deal. The swift, peeved look she gave him proved she thought it was as big a deal as he did. "What I mean," he quickly corrected himself, "is . . ." He drifted off when he realized he had no idea what he meant.

Still frowning, she wiped her fingers on her skirt, which was too drenched to dry her hands. "You need to understand, Clint—I don't do this sort of thing."

"Yeah, well, I don't make a habit of necking with women in the Pacific Ocean, either."

Her cheeks flushed again, so beautifully he had to remind himself she was seriously offended. "I don't make a habit of necking with men anywhere," she snapped.

He knew she couldn't be a man hater. No one who hated men could kiss one of the species the way she just had. He assumed that what she was saying was that she wasn't a sex maniac, which he could have guessed. "I know," he said. "You're a saint."

"I'm a human being." She tramped across the sand, holding her dripping skirt out in front of her so it wouldn't stick to her legs. "I don't know why I did what I just did with you."

"You wanted to loosen me up," he suggested, following her. He was saying all the wrong things, but he still wasn't sure what were the right things to say. Given her prickly mood, he doubted that she wanted to hear the truth: that he'd like nothing more than to take her back to Bachelor Arms, tear off her clothes and make wild and crazy love to her.

"I'm glad you think this is a joke." She gazed frantically around the beach, then pounced with relief on her abandoned sandals, which lay on the sand with Clint's shoes in a strangely intimate tangle, like lovers' shoes kicked off and abandoned on the floor beside a bed.

She bent to pick up the sandals, and when she straightened up Clint took her arm and turned her toward him. She smelled of the ocean, a deep, mysterious, womanly scent that made him want to kiss her again. "It wasn't a joke," he said.

Fortunately, she made no move to break from his light clasp. "All right, it wasn't a joke. What was it?"

He couldn't think of any answer but the truth. "It was me, wanting you."

She sighed, but what was left of her resentment seemed to drain from her. Lowering her eyes, she studied the sandy leather straps of her sandals. She ran her thumb along the tiny gold buckle where two straps intersected. The strongest, most confident woman he'd ever met had turned painfully self-conscious.

She needed reassurance. She needed to know she could be safe with him, or she would no longer be willing to spend time in his company. "Nothing more has to happen," he promised, even though the comprehension that nothing more *would* happen hurt worse than he wanted to admit.

"It's just..." She sighed again, fidgeted some more with the sandal, and at last mustered the courage to lift her gaze to his. "You'll be leaving town as soon as you find your sister. I mean, there's no—there's no purpose in this. It's just . . . I'm not built for meaningless affairs."

He wanted to swear that if they had an affair, it wouldn't be meaningless. But what she'd said was true: as soon as he found Diana he would be gone. Whatever meaning an affair with Jessie would have for him, it wouldn't be enough for her.

"I'll take you back to Rainbow House," he said, letting his hand drop from her.

She nodded and averted her gaze once more. There had been enough honesty between them for one day, for one lifetime; the honesty of their words just now, and the honesty of their kiss. She wanted him as much as he wanted her. And they were both going to be denied what they wanted. That was the sum of it.

They carried their shoes to the edge of the parking lot, tried futilely to clean the sand off their feet, then gave up and put their shoes on over the sand. Clint didn't bother donning his socks; his feet felt gritty enough without them.

He unlocked the car, but he didn't offer Jessie his hand as she got in. He was afraid that if he touched her he would kiss her again, and if he kissed her again he wouldn't be able to stop. So he only stood by, watching her arrange her wet, drooping skirt under her. When she was settled he closed her door.

She didn't look at him. Her gaze remained straight ahead. When he turned in the direction she was staring, he saw the tail end of a magnificent sunset, the sun tomato red, bleeding its color across the water's rippling surface before it ducked out of sight.

He wished his longing for Jessie would drop out of sight, too, just slip into the ocean, where the water would extinguish the flame.

Since there was no chance of that, he would simply have to put her out of his sight. He would have to search the rock clubs without her, without her knowledge to steer him and her connections to open doors for him.

He could do it. His brethren in the LAPD would help, and he could find his way back to Mace Bronson's flat if he had to, and to the recording executive, Gary Balducci.... Clint could continue his investigation without Jessie. The fact was, he hadn't even wanted her assistance in the first place.

The hell with her assistance. He'd wanted her lips on his, and he'd had her lips on his, and now he wanted a whole lot more. But he was used to losing the things he wanted. He could stand losing Jessie.

Resolution closed like a cold, hard shell around him as he took the wheel, started the engine, and drove away from the beach.

OTHER THAN PROVIDING HIM with directions back to the Santa Monica Freeway, Jessie said nothing. What could she say? That she was uncomfortably damp and chilled, that her skin stung from the residue of salt the ocean had left on it, that her skirt was ruined?

That kissing Clint McCreary had been like feeling a key slip into the lock of a secret chamber in her heart, that his kiss had awakened her to a whole new world of sensation? That he was too skeptical, too cynical, too guarded, too cold...except when he opened up and warmed up and trusted her long enough for her to fall for him?

She'd fallen, all right. She'd fallen into the water, into his lap, into his arms. She'd fallen—yet another unwelcome blush heated her cheeks as she recalled the specific part of his anatomy she'd fallen on, and how it had felt, and how much, how utterly insanely, she'd wanted to yank open the fly of his jeans and take that part of his anatomy in her hands, and...

Oh, God. This was not like her. Not at all.

Jessie was a good girl. She always had been, and always would be. She'd held on to her virginity much longer than most women did these days, not because she was a prude or a fanatic but because she was an idealist, believing that sex was too special to share with anyone she didn't absolutely love. She'd loved Danny—she'd loved him for a full year before they finally became intimate, and she'd loved him for the next year as well, and she'd still been in love with him when he'd left Los Angeles. She didn't love him anymore, but that didn't mean she was ready to go bed hopping with the first sexy man who came along.

Saint Jessie, she thought with a pang of self-loathing.

She permitted herself a quick glimpse of Clint. If his intent expression was any indication, he had nothing more on his mind than the rush-hour traffic clogging the freeway. His clothing was just as clammy as hers, his hair just as mussed, his ankles just as caked with sand. Yet he revealed not a hint of frustration over her decision to bring things to a halt between them.

Why wasn't he furious? Or hurt? Or horny? Why wasn't he busy trying to cajole her into his bed? Why wasn't he vowing on a stack of Bibles that he adored her, that he would be hers forever, that he would do anything for her if only she'd lift her skirt for him?

Why wasn't he lying to her? Wasn't that what men were supposed to do when they were trying to seduce a woman?

Obviously, Clint wasn't that kind of man. His long suit was honesty. She'd asked him what the hell had been going on between them, and he'd said, "It was me, wanting you."

It seemed clear he didn't want her anymore. Or he didn't want her enough. As long as she was acting like a wanton mermaid, kissing him with a passion that amazed her when she thought about it, he wanted her. But once she reverted to being a social worker, the director of Rainbow House, an intelligent, reasonably careful woman doing her best to survive the treacherous world of intergender relationships in the nineties, his want for her dried up a whole lot faster than his clothing.

"That's the exit," she mumbled. Her voice lacked energy, and a tremor of misery darkened it. She sounded as drippy as her hair looked.

She prayed Susan would be at Rainbow House when Clint dropped Jessie off. Susan was always good to talk things through with. If Jessie told her about the unexpected kiss, the desire that still pulsed inside her, Susan would point out that Clint wasn't Jessie's type, that he was an uptight New Yorker who didn't even know how to handle his sister, that he was a cop and cops considered her a fool for believing hard-core street kids were worth saving.

But tonight wasn't Susan's night at the shelter, so she probably wouldn't be there. If Jessie wasn't mistaken, tonight's volunteer was Mark Steinberg, a drug counselor at a private agency who also ran daytime workshops at Rainbow House. He was a great guy and an effective therapist. But Jessie couldn't picture herself sharing a cup of tea with him and pouring her heart out about the East Coast stranger she'd thrown herself at while under the influence of the sunset and the ocean and Clint's mesmerizing gray eyes.

He slowed to a stop at the end of the exit ramp. "Turn right," she reminded him.

"I know." He didn't even look at her.

She wanted to say something—if only she could think of what. That although she'd turned back his advances, she still considered him the most incredibly attractive man she'd ever met? That she was still more than willing to escort him to the clubs later tonight, if he could stand to be around her?

He didn't seem terribly receptive to anything she might have to say. He didn't seem terribly *anything*. He sat impassively, his fingers looped around the wheel, his attention on the congested streets of the neighborhood surrounding the university.

They cruised down a block of small apartments and converted houses, Clint steering carefully around bicyclists, in-line skaters, pedestrians and other cars. At the corner he let a few pedestrians cross, and then he started down the next block, slowing once more when a couple of jaywalkers darted between two parked cars in front of him. He followed them across the street with his eyes, then flinched. His foot slipped, and when he jammed his foot back down on the brake pedal Jessie lurched forward.

"What?" she gasped.

He mumbled a curse, then hit the gas and U-turned so fast the tires squealed.

"What?" Jessie asked again, bracing herself against the dashboard.

"Nothing." He tore down the street and around the corner, the outer tires momentarily leaving the pavement when he took the turn at breakneck speed.

"Clint! What are you doing? You're going to kill somebody!"

He raced down the block to the next corner, skidded to a stop, and looked left and right down the cross street. His curse this time was loud and clear.

Jessie waited a minute to make sure he wasn't going to attempt any more hot-rod maneuvers. Gingerly, she settled back in her seat, folded her hands in her lap and waited for her heartbeat to return to normal. "Would you care to explain what that was all about?"

He shook his head, but she suspected that was less a response to her question than an expression of some sort of inner bewilderment. "I thought I saw someone I recognized," he finally said.

"Your sister?" Her pulse accelerated again. If he found his sister, if there was a grand reunion and he could help put his family back together again, that would almost be enough to negate the wretchedness of the past half hour. "Did you see Diana?"

Again it took Clint a minute to answer; he was utterly lost in his own thoughts. Eventually he remembered that Jessie was in the car with him. He shook his head once more, as if he were trying to shake off something bad—a wasp circling his ear, perhaps. He looked annoyed, and pinched and a little pale.

Behind him a car honked its horn. He coasted through the intersection, pulled to the curb, and shifted into neutral. "Are you all right?" she asked.

One last shake of his head, and then he looked at her. "Sorry. It was just my imagination."

"You thought you saw your sister?"

"No, I . . ." He hesitated. His eyes took on the smoky darkness that simultaneously drew her in and warned her off. Yet he didn't order her to mind her own business. He seemed almost anxious to confide in her.

But then he thought better of it and turned away.

"You can tell me," she murmured.

"There's nothing to tell. I thought I saw someone I knew, that's all." He put the car back in gear, waited for a break in the flow of cars and merged into the traffic.

This time Clint had lied to her. She knew damned well that seeing someone he thought he knew wasn't enough to make him go pale and drive like a maniac.

He was upset about something, and it wasn't his sister. His hair was wet and his eyes were shadowed with secrets, with confusion, and if only Jessie hadn't kissed him at the beach, she might be able to help him now.

But she *had* kissed him. In those few indescribable minutes when his mouth had taken hers, and his arms had embraced her, and his hips had met hers in the warm, surging water, she had learned whether Clint would be better as a lover than as a friend. The answer wasn't the one she would have preferred.

Clint McCreary wasn't her friend, and she couldn't ask him who he'd seen or what was bothering him, or why there was nothing to tell. She couldn't do anything but sit next to him, damp and lonely and unable to connect with him. She couldn't do anything but let him drive her back to Rainbow House.

When they reached the rehabilitated frat house, she got out of the car. He reached across the seat from inside to close it. Through the open passenger window his eyes met hers, just as they had the first time she'd seen him, that morning near the Civic Center. Her heart twinged the way it had then, and her hands ached to touch his, to close around his and hold on tight.

But she'd already pushed him away. Changing her mind now, inviting him in, wrapping him in her arms and begging him to make the ache disappear... She couldn't do it.

All she could do was watch him drive down the street and out of sight.

7

CLINT SAT IN AN ORNATE wrought-iron chair on the patio
abutting the Bachelor Arms building. The courtyard
struck him as very Californian—patterned concrete,
tropical plants, a vast cemented-over swimming pool.
He could imagine giddy Busby-Berkley chorines bouncing around in the pool sixty-odd years ago, more daring
in their modest swimsuits than the ladies in the bikinis
at Santa Monica State Beach were that afternoon. He
could imagine suave movie stars, all those pretty-boy
actors of yore whose photographs graced the walls of
Flynn's, lounging about the pool in satin-trimmed beach
robes, smoking cigarettes through long ebony cigarette
holders and ogling the young lovelies in the water.

There were no young lovelies, no pretty boys on the
patio right now. Only Clint, clutching a frosty bottle of
beer, listening to the distant drone of traffic on Wilshire
Boulevard and the rustle of night breezes sifting through
the palm fronds. Above him the sky was purple velvet,
thick and warm. He was cold, though, colder than the
bottle in his hand. And it had nothing to do with the
weather.

He was looking for someone. His sister. A dirtbag
named Jocko. A mysterious woman with porcelain skin
and sable hair, who had somehow made her face appear
in his mirror one evening in an inexplicable attempt to
drive him insane.

He was looking for all of them. But most of all, he was looking for Jessie.

Jessie. Cripes, he didn't have to look for her. He knew where she was, how to find her, how to see her again. The only thing he didn't know was what the hell he was supposed to do once he was with her.

He knew what he wanted to do. He wanted to take her in his arms and never let go. He wanted to kiss her. He wanted to stroke his tongue along the silky underside of her jaw, and fill his hands with her breasts. He wanted to wrap her legs around him and bury himself inside her. He wanted to hear her moan. He wanted to feel her come.

And that, of course, was why he was sitting alone in this California courtyard, sucking down a beer and feeling sorry for himself.

He should have been club hopping, journeying from joint to joint in search of Jocko and Diana. But he couldn't imagine doing the club scene all by himself.

He didn't go to clubs back home. He preferred listening to music somewhere where he didn't have to yell above the din to have a conversation. And he didn't like pickup venues, places where you met a woman, shouted at her for a half hour, and went back to her place or yours.

He loved sex. He loved waking up to find someone soft and pretty beside him in the morning. But when you took a woman home with you, even if you both understood it was for one night, she assumed she had a right to a certain closeness with you. Not just physical closeness, but emotional. Maybe she deserved that closeness, maybe by giving you entry to her body she earned entry to your soul. But Clint didn't want anyone burrowing into his psyche. That was where he hid his hurts and his scars, and he didn't share them with anybody.

Dysfunctional, he thought with a snort. Where the hell did Jessie get off labeling his family with her glib clinical terminology? His was a good family, a decent family, cemented by love. If anything was dysfunctional, it was the society that had destroyed his family for a few bucks and the fun of it.

The sound of a man's baritone chuckle broke into his thoughts. A woman responded in a Dixie drawl. Clint recognized the woman's voice; it belonged to the waitress from Flynn's who had told him about the available apartment in Bachelor Arms. Given the flirting tone in the man's laughter, Clint assumed he must be her boyfriend.

The laughter faded behind the closing of a door, and he heard footsteps across the courtyard. He took a long drink from his bottle and kept his gaze riveted on the swimming pool. He wasn't in the mood to be sociable with a waitress and her boyfriend.

The footsteps drew closer, and Clint realized only one person had ventured into the courtyard—the man, judging by the heavy tread. Sighing, Clint contemplated whether to make a quick departure or stick around and deal with the intruder. He didn't want to go back inside and spend what was left of the evening staring at the mirror in his living room, but he wasn't in the mood to engage in superficial chitchat with a stranger, either.

Before he could make up his mind, the man appeared beside Clint's chair, smiling down at him. "Well, well, what have we here?" he said, a bit too heartily.

Clint gazed up at the man. He was good-looking, in his midforties or thereabouts, impeccably barbered, neatly mustached and dressed to kill. What Clint knew about fashion could be summed up in three words: *jeans and shirts.* He was conscious enough, however, to recognize that the man's jacket and trousers must have cost a bundle.

"Anything I can help you with?" the man asked, sounding suspicious.

"No, thanks."

"This courtyard is for the use of Bachelor Arms residents only. I don't know how you—"

"I'm a resident."

"Oh. No problem, then." The man smiled, angled his head and studied Clint thoughtfully, then wagged his finger in an I-know-who-you-are manner. "You're 1-G, aren't you?"

"No," Clint said with fake affability. "My apartment is 1-G."

"Bobbie-Sue was just telling me someone moved in." The man extended his right hand. "Theodore Smith. Welcome to Bachelor Arms."

Clint had no choice but to shake hands with him. "Clint McCreary."

Unfortunately, Clint's perfunctory courtesy encouraged Theodore Smith to join him. He settled into a chair facing Clint, hitching his impeccable trousers at the knee and crossing one leg over the other thigh. His leather loafers had impractical thin soles. The sleeves of his blazer were cuffed, and under it he wore what appeared to be a silk T-shirt.

He regarded Clint with a combination of curiosity and distrust. "So, Clint . . . Welcome to Bachelor Arms."

Clint managed another impassive smile, and took a sip of his beer.

"Have you seen her?" Theodore asked.

"The ghost?" Clint sized up Mr. Fancy-Pants, wondering if he was the perpetrator of the practical joke. "No," he lied, figuring that if word got out that he hadn't seen the woman in the mirror, whoever was behind the gag might try to pull it off a second time.

"Neither have I," Theodore admitted. "Which, frankly, is just fine with me. Enough of my dreams have come true to make me think that if I saw her, I wouldn't get my greatest hope—I'd get my greatest fear. It took guts for you to rent that apartment, Clint. The last tenant—"

"I heard. He saw her and ran away."

"At least she hasn't scared you away yet." Theodore leaned back in his chair, settling in for a long stay. Clint tried to figure out a tactful way to get up and leave. "Where are you from?"

"New York City," he answered brusquely.

"Really?" Theodore seemed completely oblivious to Clint's lack of enthusiasm for their conversation. Nothing the guy had said or done would have bothered Clint if he hadn't been so keyed up about Jessie. "I love that town. Life there is something else."

Clint stared at him in stony silence.

"I'm talking about the *ladies*," Theodore explained. "They're harder to get through to than the babes out here in La-La Land, but hey, I'm the sort of guy who likes to rise to the challenge, no pun intended."

Clint forced a smile.

"They're smart, New York ladies. They lead with their mouths. Not like in L.A. Here they lead with their eyes, give you the once-over, and if you pass inspection you're in. Know what I mean?"

Clint doubted the women in Los Angeles were that shallow. Jessie certainly wasn't. He was pretty sure he'd passed her inspection, but he was definitely out with her.

"It helps if a guy keeps his threads in working order," Theodore added, giving Clint's casual attire a supercilious assessment as he adjusted his well-cut jacket, which needed no adjusting. "I ought to know, being as I work at Aldus."

"Aldus." Clint drew a blank.

"One of the better apparel shops." Theodore gave Clint a close scrutiny. "Listen, my friend, your wardrobe could use a bit of touching up, but not to worry. The odds are in your favor out here. Right here in this very building, I'll tell you ... There's Bobbie-Sue, who's a bit on the chilly side, but merely looking at her is a joy in itself. And her best friend Brenda— Have you met Brenda yet?"

Clint shook his head and drank some beer.

"And then there's Jill Foyle who I had the pleasure of dating once. It didn't work out for some reason. Of course, she's a bit older—relatively speaking—but I'm sure if the right man with the right line came along, she could be had. They're all here, Clint, just waiting for us."

Clint entertained a brief fantasy of aiming his fist about an inch above Theodore's mustache and letting it fly. He had his share of sexist notions, but damn it, he didn't like men talking about women as if they were pieces of fruit to be tasted and then discarded.

He kept his annoyance to himself. Theodore Smith wasn't someone Clint would seek out for friendship, but he was here, available and eager to talk. And Clint was enough of an investigator not to waste the opportunity Theodore presented. "I bet you make the rounds of the clubs a lot," he said.

"Clubs? Dance places, you mean?"

"Live-music places. Rock clubs."

"Rock." Theodore winced. "Not my favorite music, I'm afraid. Put a gorgeous woman in my arms and play some Tony Bennett in the background, and I'll think I've died and gone to heaven. But rock . . ." He scowled. "It's all bang-bang-bang. Migraine music, I call it."

"Yeah, well . . ." Clint gave Theodore an ingratiating smile. "I always heard the clubs out in L.A. were pretty cutting edge. I just thought, while I was in town I ought to check out the action."

"I understand a man can strike up some very interesting acquaintances in those clubs. Lots of dancing with lots of ladies. Sure, I've made the rounds. Not to listen, but to make acquaintances."

"Mmm." Some overheated creep like Theodore could right this minute be making Diana's acquaintance at a club while Jocko was up on stage. The possibility did not please Clint. "I've heard there's a real Romeo who does the clubs, a rock star himself, very hot at the moment. Goes by the name Jocko."

"Jocko?" Theodore guffawed. "Well, there's a name for you. *Jocko*. I guess rockers like to choose their own handles. When was the last time you heard of a rock star named, oh, say, Stanley? Or Bartholomew, you know? It's got to be cool. Sting. Slash. *Jocko*."

"Have you ever heard of him?"

"Jocko." Theodore mulled over the name. Perhaps he was trying to appear thoughtful, but in truth he looked pained, his polished face scrunched into a grimace of concentration. "Jocko . . ."

"Never mind." Clint wasn't getting anywhere with this guy, and his beer bottle was empty. At last he had a reasonable excuse to leave the courtyard. "It looks like I've run dry here," he said, displaying the bottle and rising to his feet. He smiled politely. "Nice meeting you."

"You know, there's one club I've heard of—a lady I used to see hung out there a lot. They were always showcasing new bands. Every night was open-mike night. Damn, what was the name of that place?"

Clint hovered near his chair. He was utterly ignorant when it came to the rock scene in Los Angeles. Like a starving man, he would devour any scrap Theodore tossed him.

"Rumble, or something."

"Rumble?"

"Thunder. That was it. Thunder. It was just off the Strip, a basement place. She took me there once. Migraine City."

"Thanks," Clint said, meaning it. *Thunder.* If the club showcased new bands, the manager might know Jocko, or even Mace Bronson. The bouncer might have seen Diana coming and going. It could be a lead.

Or it could be a dead end.

Even so, if what Theodore had given Clint was nothing, it was still more than he'd had before. He reached out and gave Theodore's hand a genuine shake. "Thanks, pal. I appreciate the information."

"Listen, Clint, if you want someone to make the rounds with, count me in. Who cares what they're playing, as long as you've got someone pretty and willing to play with you, right?"

"I'll keep you in mind." Clint tipped his bottle toward Theodore in a would-be toast, then strolled into the building, feeling invigorated. If Thunder was off Sunset Strip, he could probably find it. How many basement rock clubs could there be in that relatively short stretch of Sunset Boulevard? How many open-mike places?

He'd visit them all. He'd start with Thunder and proceed from there.

Entering his apartment, he avoided glancing in the direction of the mirror. Not because he was spooked, not because he believed that a woman he'd seen strolling along a street near Rainbow House a few hours ago could possibly materialize in the silver glass, but because the thing was so oppressively ugly.

The trouble was, when he directed his gaze away from the mirror, it landed on the writing desk, where Jessie's card sat.

He didn't want to go to Thunder without her. He didn't want to do anything without her.

He couldn't call her. If he heard her voice, he'd want her. Even *not* hearing her voice, he wanted her. Just seeing her card turned him on, seeing her name in letters, remembering the heat of her mouth on his, her body, her helpless moan as the tide rushed in around them . . .

He'd go to the club without her. Period.

Less than a minute later, he was dialing her number.

"I HOPE YOU DON'T MIND my calling you at home," he said.

Jessie carried the cordless receiver to the living room and sank into her favorite easy chair. She'd bought it used when she'd signed a lease for this apartment, one of twenty in an art deco motel that had been converted into rental units. Except for the mattress on her bed, all her furniture had been bought used. It was comfortable stuff, mismatched but indestructible, and she'd spent numerous weekends recovering the upholstery and refinishing the tables. For an apartment decorated on a shoestring budget, Jessie had done an excellent job.

The furniture might have been accumulated on the cheap, but she spent real money on the important things: her stereo system, her VCR, and her cordless telephone. Different calls required different environments, and she wanted to be free to move around while she was on the phone. She talked to her mother in the kitchenette; she made work calls from the battered oak rolltop desk in the corner. A call from Clint tempted her to carry the phone into her bedroom, but she had a strong enough sense of self-preservation to remain in the living room.

Even so, the chair's plush cushions seemed to embrace her like a lover's arms, sending a thick, heavy heat down into her body as she cradled the receiver and pictured Clint at the other end of the connection. Hell, it wasn't the cushions that made her feel embraced. It was the low, dark sound of his voice, and the memory of his kiss, his body pressed to hers.

"I called the shelter, and a guy there—Mark Something-or-Other—gave me your number."

"He shouldn't have done that," Jessie murmured, although she knew there was no danger in Mark's giving her home number to Clint. At least, not the usual danger.

"Don't give him a hard time. I finessed him."

Once again, Jessie reminded herself that Clint had been a cop. No doubt he was a professional at wheedling information from strangers.

How he got her home telephone number didn't matter, she reminded herself. The fact was, he was on the phone with her, and she wished he were in the room with her. She wished she could be gazing into his eyes and feeling his mouth on hers again, feeling his hands stroking the length of her back, feeling his hips nestled against hers.

His having her home phone number was *definitely* a dangerous thing.

"I heard about a rock club," he was saying. "One of my neighbors mentioned it. It's called Thunder, just off Sunset Strip."

"I know the place." It was a low-rent joint, not one of the pricey, semiprivate clubs where showbiz people went. She and Susan had gone to Thunder a few times. The drinks had been watered down and the bands had been underrehearsed, but the clientele had been salt of the earth, and she'd had a good time.

"I don't even know where to begin with these clubs," Clint confessed. "I'm sure there are hundreds of them. I just thought, maybe I should get my butt in gear and start checking them out. Somebody someplace might know something."

"I agree," she said. The sooner he found his sister, the sooner he would be gone from L.A., and the sooner she could get him out of her system.

"I'd like you to come with me." No wheedling now, no finesse. He hadn't even phrased the request as a question. He'd simply stated his wishes.

If she simply stated hers, she'd say yes. But if she went to Thunder with him, she would spend the night in the hypnotic glow of his bedroom eyes. He would take her arm as she got in and out of his car, and his touch would ignite treacherous yearnings inside her.

She'd stopped kissing him at the beach because she'd known she had to. But she hadn't stopped desiring him.

"I don't think that's a good idea, Clint," she said now.

"Jessie. You could really help me out here. You know this club, you probably know others...." He exhaled. "If you're worried about us being together... I told you this afternoon, nothing more has to happen."

But she *wanted* more to happen. That was the whole problem.

Her silence prompted him to continue. "I know it sounds like a cliché, but I respect you. I don't want to mess up your life. One-night stands aren't my style, either. I'm asking you, one friend to another, to visit a couple of clubs with me. Okay?"

"Clint." She sounded plaintive to herself, moved by his plainspoken honesty. Maybe he *could* be a friend as well as a lover. Even if she couldn't trust herself, she could certainly trust him. But . . .

"If you're not with me when I meet Jocko," he added, "I'm going to tear his head off. I need you with me to make me behave."

Now he was wheedling—with such easy self-mockery she laughed. Her laughter washed away the last of her hesitation. "You *would* tear his head off, wouldn't you?"

"With my bare hands."

"All right," she relented. "I'll go to Thunder with you. And I'll point out some of the other clubs for you. But that's all. I don't want to go club hopping tonight." It wasn't yet nine o'clock, and she had no early-morning appointments tomorrow, but she felt it necessary to establish certain boundaries before she saw Clint again.

"Where do you live?" he asked.

"Just off Wilshire Boulevard. If you're heading toward Westwood, about a half mile past Hawthorne—"

"No kidding? We're neighbors, Jessie."

"We are?"

"I live on Wilshire. Do you know a bar called Flynn's?"

"Sure, I know Flynn's."

"Well, there's this weird pink house next door—"

"You live in that house? I love that house! I've driven past it a million times." It was one of those grand old mansions that proclaimed Hollywood's glamorous past, just as the streamlined deco architecture of the converted motel where she lived also recalled Hollywood's Golden Age. "How can you live in such a palace?" she asked, suddenly skeptical. An ex-cop from New York didn't just pop into town and buy an estate on Wilshire Boulevard.

"It's divided into apartments now," he explained. "I was able to score a one-month lease on one of the units."

"Well, I've adored that building from the first time I saw it. Why do you call it weird?"

He meditated for a long minute before answering. "I guess New Yorkers aren't used to pink houses with turquoise trim." He fell silent again, and she was sure he had more to say on the subject of the house's alleged weirdness. He thought better of it, though. "I'll need your exact address."

"Maybe I ought to drive. I know the Strip better than you do."

"Yeah, but . . . don't you think doing the club scene in a van is a little tacky?"

No, she didn't. She had often gone to clubs, video arcades and any of a number of other teenage hangouts in her van, searching for misplaced youngsters in need of the kind of help Rainbow House offered. But Clint evidently had an aversion to vans. "If you want to drive, fine," she conceded, then gave him her address.

He promised to pick her up in a half hour, and they said goodbye. Jessie pressed the disconnect button on her handset and sighed, partly with pleasure at the thought of seeing Clint again, and partly with disgust at herself.

If she saw him, she was going to remember the kiss. She was going to relive the passion that had scrambled her brain and made her behave recklessly with him.

She was going to want to behave recklessly again.

She wasn't an idiot, though—her willingness to go club hopping with him notwithstanding. She had agreed to take him to Thunder, and whatever other clubs he wanted to visit, because the sooner he found his sister the sooner he would be out of Jessie's life. Really, seeing him tonight was a good way to get rid of him.

Just to be sure he wouldn't misconstrue the situation, she groomed carefully. After showering, she dressed in old, comfortable black jeans, a pale blue pocket T-shirt, and canvas high-tops. She braided her hair out of her face and donned her gold hoop earrings. The clothing and the hairdo made her look younger than her age, which was an asset if she wanted to fit in with the kids hanging out at Thunder. She certainly wouldn't be mistaken—by Clint or anyone else—for a woman on the make.

She had just finished stuffing a small wallet into her pocket when Clint rang her bell. All the speeches she'd given herself during the past thirty minutes—the one about how he was only a human being, perfectly resistible, and the one about how, unlike the troubled kids she worked with, Clint had no interest in being saved by her, and the one about how Clint lived on the other side of the country and the other end of the spectrum—evaporated into nothingness as she opened the door to him.

Like her, he'd dressed down, in jeans and a loose-fitting T-shirt. His hair was arranged casually, still slightly damp from the shower, and his mouth was curved in a tentative smile. "All set to go?" he asked, loitering just outside her front door as if afraid of what might happen if he stepped inside.

Jessie shared that fear. "All set," she said brightly, joining him on the front porch and locking up before she could change her mind and invite him in.

She remained a discreet distance from him as they walked to the parking lot at the center of the horseshoe-shaped building. Clint's gaze skidded from the fragrant lemon tree beside the front walk to the gaudy hibiscus bordering the lot, to the glittering blue pool at the apex of the horseshoe. "This looks almost like a hotel," he said.

"It used to be one," she told him. "Until the midsixties, I gather."

"Everything is so low here." He glanced at the arching two-story building. "Except for downtown L.A., all the buildings seem so low. I can't get used to it."

"That's because of the earthquakes," she explained. "They say the skyscrapers downtown are earthquake-proof, if you want to believe that. As for me, I prefer the low buildings to all the towers in New York City. Here, at least, you can see the sky."

"You can see the smog."

"Oh, and New York has no air pollution," she teased.

"It's not as bad as Los Angeles."

She liked sparring with him. "In New York," she declared, "the air is polluted with such foreign objects as snow and ice. I'll take soot over sleet any day."

"Hypothermia is a comfortable way to die, especially compared to emphysema," he said pointedly.

She wanted to win the argument, but laughter was bubbling up inside her. Once she let it out, of course, she felt obligated to concede defeat. "All right, Clint—when it's time for me to die, I'll try to freeze instead of wheeze."

"It pays to plan ahead," he said dryly, then succumbed to his own laughter.

If they could keep laughing like this, she was going to survive the evening. Enjoy it, even. She was going to relax and have a good time bopping from club to club with him, asking people about his sister and Jocko. They'd endure the noise and squalor with their senses of humor and their camaraderie. They would get through this without breaking into a sweat.

"Turn left at the corner," she instructed him. "First stop, Thunder."

8

THE BASEMENT CLUB was dark, smoky, crowded and noisy—everything a successful rock club was supposed to be. Once he'd paid the cover charge, Clint took Jessie's hand and led her into the dimly lit cellar room. She knew he was holding hands with her only so he wouldn't lose track of her in the zero-visibility mob scene. His clasp wasn't anything personal. She had already made it clear to him that afternoon that nothing romantic was going to develop between them.

That his fingers were just a bit too strong as he wove them through hers, just a bit too thick, too confoundedly masculine . . . that the warmth of his grip spread up her arm and into her body, inundating her flesh and filling her mind with images of his hands elsewhere on her, touching, arousing . . . that she couldn't hold hands with him without reacting in an embarrassingly sexual way was her problem, not his.

At the far end of the room, a band no more than a month past the garage rehearsal phase was performing. Banks of amplifiers blasted the music into the air, making conversation difficult at best. Voices swirled around her in a muddle; the clinks of glasses and bottles blended with the stomps of kids in Doc Martens boots dancing on the scuffed floor at the center of the room.

As she and Clint moved deeper into the crowd, she could barely keep him in her sight, so she held his hand tighter. He blazed a path through the forest of bodies, weaving adroitly around tables she didn't even see until she was about to collide with them. Either he was mercilessly elbowing his way through the hordes, or else the rock fans saw something in his face, felt something in his presence that made them willing to step back and let him pass.

He led Jessie to a clearing with a view of the dance floor and the two-inch platform that served as a stage. The band looked stereotypically mangy, the female lead singer dressed in tattered lace and the other musicians sporting defiantly antiuniform uniforms—patched jeans, ragged shirts, vests and unidentified dangling objects on leather cords around their necks. A sign propped against one tower of amps read Chicken Livers.

"I guess that's the name of the band," Jessie remarked.

Clint frowned, unable to hear her. He bent his head and she rose on tiptoe so she could repeat her comment directly into his ear. Instinctively she hooked her hand over his shoulder to keep her balance. Her lungs filled with the spicy scent of his shampoo, and her fingers flexed against the sturdy muscles of his back.

Touching him forced her to remember his kiss at the beach that afternoon, his powerful embrace, the feel of his lean, hard body beneath her as the warm saltwater whirled around them. She remembered it all, every moment of it, every beat of her heart, every pleading sigh of her soul. Merely his proximity made everything—his blatant sexuality and her own helpless reaction to him—much too vivid.

"Chicken Livers," he grunted, dragging her back to the present. "Stupid name."

"It's appropriate. I like their music about as much as I like liver," she said.

He grinned and nodded. "None of them looks like a Jocko to me."

"Well, what were the odds that he would just happen to be playing here tonight?"

Clint nodded again. "In a few minutes we can mosey around, ask the bartenders if they know his name."

This time she nodded. It was easier than shouting— and safer than pulling herself against him to speak into his ear again.

The band concluded a song that seemed to be about ingrown toenails as a metaphor for existential angst. A waitress in a leotard and baggy overalls came over and asked if they wanted drinks. Before they could answer, the waitress vanished.

"I wasn't thirsty, anyway," Jessie said with a grin. "Do you like rock music?"

"The real thing," Clint answered. "Not this stuff."

"What's the real thing?"

A wry smile twisted his lips. "The Police, of course."

She laughed. "You must like more than one band."

"I like the stuff that was in when I was their age," he said, waving vaguely at the college-age kids around them. "I'm an old man, now, with old tastes. Springsteen, Mellencamp, Bonnie Raitt—the oldies."

"They aren't such oldies," she argued. If those musicians were old-timers, then she must be pretty old herself. "You can dance to this music, at least."

He shrugged. "I'm not a dancer."

She could have guessed as much. To enjoy dancing, a person had to be able to let go and shoo the shadows away for a while. The only time Clint had let go, the only time she'd seen the shadows disappear from his eyes, had been when he'd kissed her.

And she'd put those shadows right back into his eyes, hadn't she?

Someone in the crowd to her left was calling her name. She turned to search the throng, and Paul Gaskin's familiar face caught her eye. Paul was an English teacher at Beverly Hills High School. He and Jessie had met a couple of years ago at an all-day workshop on troubled adolescents, and since then he'd invited her to address his classes every spring on the dangers of the streets and the alternatives to running away from home. He and Jessie often joked about their contrasting taste in music; he liked rock bands so young and green she'd never even heard of them, while she, fifteen years his junior, preferred rock that predated even Clint's favorite music: the Beach Boys, of course, and the Beatles, the Lovin' Spoonful, all those peace-love-and-flowers bands whose careers had peaked before she was born.

"Hello, stranger!" Paul hollered, maneuvering his way through the crowd to her. "Slumming it, are you?"

"I could accuse you of the same thing."

Paul smiled and extended his hand to Clint, who regarded Paul intently. The bald, stocky Paul definitely didn't seem the type—or the age—to frequent clubs like Thunder. Chicken Livers' lead guitarist strummed a tortured, reverberating chord, and Jessie had to shout introductions between the two men. Paul tried to ask Clint something; Clint shook his head, unable to hear.

The band kicked in with a new song. "Wanna boogie?" Paul asked Jessie.

She wanted to dance with Clint, but he would never ask her, so she accepted Paul's invitation with a smile.

Shouting to Clint that she would be back soon, she accompanied Paul out onto the floor.

It occurred to her that while she and Paul were dancing, Clint might vanish into the throng. He might prefer
to interrogate the barmaids and bouncers without her
tagging along. Or, even though he'd told her he wasn't a
dancer, he might ask someone else to join him on the
dance floor. It was possible that he might enjoy dancing
just fine; he just didn't want to dance with *her*.

She shot a glance in his direction and saw him at the
edge of the dance floor, his gaze riveted on her, his expression mirthless. Was he angry? Jealous? Or just annoyed that she was wasting precious time dancing with
Paul when she was supposed to be helping Clint find his
sister?

Let him stew, she thought, turning back to Paul and
grinning as he gyrated his middle-aged body in time to
the band's song. Let Clint simmer and seethe on the
sidelines. If he wanted to dance with her, he could
damned well ask her. And if he didn't, she would dance
with a fun-loving friend.

The song wound down with a clatter of percussion,
and the room became relatively less noisy. "Thanks,"
Jessie said, sharing a smile with Paul.

"My pleasure. So, how are things in Oz?"

For a moment, she thought he was speaking of Oz as
that fantastical place where she could drop her inhibitions and Clint could drop his grim reticence and they
could finish what they'd begun at the beach. But then she
realized Paul was referring to Rainbow House. "Same as
always," she told him. "Busier than I'd like."

The bassist retuned his guitar, the deep notes causing the floor to vibrate under Jessie's feet. Paul seemed on the verge of speaking, but obviously thought better of it.

Suddenly Clint loomed into view. She hadn't seen him step out onto the dance floor, yet there he was, edging around Paul and sidling up to Jessie.

"The next dance is mine," he said. Although his voice was low, she had no trouble hearing him.

Paul smiled affably and moved aside. Jessie was less inclined to give in to Clint so quickly. "Are you asking me or telling me?"

He gazed at her, his eyes glinting in the subdued light. He was asking *and* telling, she comprehended—telling her he wanted her, asking her if she wanted him.

They had come here to look for his sister and Jocko, hadn't they? Their moment of madness at the beach was long past. This evening's outing wasn't supposed to be about anyone wanting anyone.

The band started another song, and Clint closed his hand around hers, depriving her of the chance to turn him down—a chance she wouldn't have taken, anyway. She *did* want Clint, no matter how many times she told herself she shouldn't want him. In her work, Jessie always trusted her heart over her brain, and her heart had never misled her. Right now it was crying out that she should trust Clint, accept him, accept her own desires.

She prayed it wasn't misleading her this time.

For heaven's sake, it was only a dance! There was no need for her to get caught up in the emotional undertow. She could simply take a spin on the dance floor with Clint and not turn it into a major emotional crisis.

She sent a farewell smile to Paul, who was already hooking up with another woman from the crowd on the dance floor. The lace-clad lead singer wailed, in an unfortunately slow blues tempo.

Clint pulled Jessie into his arms.

"I thought you didn't like to dance," she said, talking to distract herself from the seductive nearness of his body, the possessiveness of his arm around her.

"I don't."

"Then why are we dancing?"

He let his hand drift up her back to the nape of her neck. Feathery wisps of hair had unraveled from her braid, and he toyed with them, his fingertips brushing against her skin and sending shivers of heat down her spine.

"I saw you dancing with your friend, and I thought, why him?"

"Paul and I go way back," she explained, amazed that her voice emerged calmly while ripples of longing continued to descend through her flesh. "As they say in Hollywood—" she grinned "— we're just friends."

"The question wasn't, why *him*," Clint clarified. "It was, why not *me*?"

"Well, I guess it *is* you. I mean, here we are, dancing."

"Yeah," Clint said, bringing his hand back down to her waist and drawing her closer to him. "Here we are, dancing."

"Maybe after this dance we ought to start asking about Diana." *Because if we don't focus on her soon, I'm going to forget all the reasons I don't want your arms around me like this.*

"Sure." He pulled her even closer.

"Clint." Her voice no longer sounded calm. His name emerged as a gasp, which wasn't terribly surprising, since having his body so close to hers was making her breath-

less. Not that she minded the way the sheer male strength
of his physique caused her breasts to tingle and her legs
to feel shaky, the way his leanly muscled chest cushioned hers and his knees nudged hers. Not that she
minded in the least being rendered breathless by Clint.

She rested her head on his shoulder and clung more
snugly to him, telling herself that if she didn't she would
probably lose her balance—but knowing that she was
clinging to him because she wanted to, because he felt
good, because her heart was overriding her brain and her
heart told her this was right.

"What a song," Jessie murmured, afraid to say what
she was really thinking: that Clint's body fit hers perfectly. That his shoulder was so firm, so strong, and his
arm spanned her waist so comfortably, and her hips felt
magnetized by his.

"I wouldn't call it a song," Clint murmured back,
shifting so his lips were near her ear. His breath caressed
her earlobe and the sensitive skin of her throat.

"What would you call it?" She wondered if he could
hear the tremor in her voice as his hand caressed her
waist, easing her even closer to him, guiding her hips
more intimately against his. Through the layers of denim
that separated their bodies she felt his hardness. Her
arousal matched his, a thick, fluid heat gathering below
her belly. She had to bite her lip to keep from moaning
as sensation flooded her.

"I'd call it crap." Despite the laughter in his voice, it
was dark and husky, as if he'd just confessed his most
private secret.

No longer pretending to dance, he stopped moving his
feet. As if he took the term *rock music* literally, he rocked
against her in an insinuating rhythm that made her ache.

Jessie was burning, burning up in Clint's sensual embrace. She imagined him branding her, staking his claim upon her, leaving his mark deep within her—and even if she would ultimately be left with scars, it seemed...inevitable.

She lifted her head from his shoulder and tilted it upward. He bowed and covered her mouth with his, as if he, too, saw no point in fighting the inevitable.

She parted her lips and lured him into her mouth. His tongue slid over hers, tangled with it, surged and retreated and surged again. His hand curved around her bottom and held her steady, and his hips surged and retreated in tandem with his tongue.

It was like making love with their clothes on.

Breaking the kiss, she sucked in a tremulous breath and closed her eyes. "Let's leave," she whispered.

"Yeah," he agreed, sounding just as shaken, just as breathless.

It took several prolonged minutes for them to find the will to loosen their holds on each other. As Clint relaxed his embrace Jessie felt the soreness in knees too wobbly to hold her up, in thighs that had clenched and arched her against him. Her lips felt sore, too, her breasts heavy and tender.

If she brought him back to her bed tonight, she was going to feel a hell of a lot sorer tomorrow, or the next day, or whenever the fateful moment arrived for Clint to say goodbye. She had no doubt that it would arrive, sooner or later. Probably sooner.

He was going to break her heart. He was going to leave her burned and scarred and bleeding...and she couldn't stop wanting him. Jessie—the good girl, the Wizard, the saint—didn't care.

Clint kept one arm draped around her shoulders as they made their way awkwardly through the crowd. They inched around clusters of people, sidestepped dancers, avoided tables and rushing waitresses. Near the bar, Jessie spotted Paul and his new dance partner, and she exchanged a wave with him. She wondered if he could read the future in her smile—the immediate, *tonight* future and the other future, the one she didn't want to face until she had to.

Near the door the crowd was thick. The band had announced a ten-minute break between sets, and a bottleneck was forming as patrons prepared for a migration to the next club, where perhaps the band wasn't on a break. Clint took advantage of the traffic jam to turn Jessie in his arms and kiss her again.

His eyes were as dark as the night. She saw passion in them, hunger . . . and more. Something that could have been sorrow. Something that could have been fear.

We don't have to do this, she nearly said—except that it wouldn't be true. Somehow, she sensed, they *did* have to do this. If they didn't . . .

If they didn't, logic sternly informed her, she'd wind up a lot better off.

But then his lips touched hers again, melted hers, coaxed hers apart, and being better off didn't seem so terribly important.

"Jocko," someone in the crowd said.

She was sure she'd misheard. But if she had, so had Clint. His hands fell still on her waist and he lifted his face from hers and frowned.

"Someone's talking about him," he said.

"I know."

Pulling away from her, he scanned the sea of unlit faces. So did Jessie. It had sounded like a man's voice, but many of the men in the club had long hair and earrings and young faces, and the room was so dark—

"And she's, like, 'Jocko's so cool,' and I'm like—"

"It could be a different Jocko," Jessie noted.

Ignoring her warning, Clint let go of her and nudged his way through the mass of people, hot on the trail of the voice.

Jessie followed him, repeatedly muttering, "Excuse me, excuse me," for both herself and Clint, who was too intent to waste time on etiquette.

In a knot of people huddling near the steps to the door, he latched on to a young man. "Who's Jocko?" he growled.

"Huh?" The kid looked terrified. His hair was a carrot red mop, and he wore a gold wire through his pierced upper lip. His eyes widened as he gazed up at Clint.

"I just heard you talking about someone named Jocko."

"Not me, man."

Clint's fingers tightened around the kid's arm. "I heard you."

"*Giacomo*," the kid said. "I was talking about *Giacomo*."

Jessie tried to pry Clint away from the kid. Obviously he was talking about someone else; Clint had no right to badger him. But he persisted, hanging on to the kid's arm. "Giacomo who?"

"I don't know his last name. He's just called Giacomo, that's all. You know, like Cher. Or Madonna, or something."

"Who is he?"

"He's this...I dunno. This rock star from Italy or something. I dunno. My girl left me for him."

Clint's grip relented, but his intensity increased. "I'm looking for a girl who left her boyfriend for Giacomo. Does he collect girls?"

"Yeah." All of a sudden, the kid and Clint were buddies, allied against the girl-collecting Giacomo. "The dude's slick, man. Slick and rich. They say he made tons of money as a rock star in Italy, but he doesn't do music here. He just steals girls."

"Do you know where he lives?"

"Beverly Hills somewhere. Just off Mulholland."

"I been there," a friend of the kid's joined in. "He does parties."

"What's his address?"

"Man, I don't know." The kid named a street. "Big Spanish house on a corner, with a circular driveway and a pool out back. I guess that sounds like half the houses there, but..." He struggled to remember the number. "You know what I remember about it? His mailbox, you know? Up by the driveway? He had a rooster painted on it."

"A rooster." Clint's voice was taut. Jessie knew he was furious. She couldn't blame him. The connotations of a rooster—the one male among a harem of hens—wasn't pleasant.

Clint contained his rage, though. The hand that had gripped the first boy now patted his shoulder in gratitude. "Thanks, bud," he said.

"You know what I think?" The boy swaggered. "Any girl who runs off with a toad like Giacomo? She isn't worth it, man."

"You're right," Clint said, even though Jessie knew he didn't mean it. He'd said it to make the kid feel better about losing his girlfriend to Giacomo.

She and Clint made their meandering way through the crowd, up the stairs and out onto the street. The night air felt cool after the stuffy atmosphere of the club, and strangely still after all the clanging, nerve-jarring noise of bad music and screeching voices.

Jessie drew in a deep breath of fresh air and waited for her head to stop pounding. Next to her Clint brooded. He stuffed his hands into his pockets and gazed at her, his expression unreadable.

Just five minutes ago, they'd been leaving the club with the intention of making love. Now she knew that was impossible. She ought to have been grateful that fate had stepped in and saved her when she'd been too swept away to save herself.

She *was* grateful, she swore to herself. She'd just dodged a bullet; she ought to race back inside and thank the kid as sincerely as Clint had.

But she wasn't happy. She felt strangely empty, wistful, the way a child feels when her mother stops her from making herself sick with candy or riding her bike without a helmet. Yes, it was better not to get a tummy ache or a concussion. But the exhilarating freedom of riding a bicycle with the wind in her hair, the crazy indulgence of stuffing her mouth with sugary goodies...

Jessie couldn't help thinking that maybe, for once in her life, she'd have been better sorry than safe.

She studied Clint's face, unable to tell whether what she saw in his eyes was disappointment or relief, or perhaps a combination of both. He started to speak, then changed his mind and pressed his lips together. Those lips had taken hers just minutes ago. Those lips had danced across her brow, had brushed the edge of her ear, had conquered her mouth and whispered that he was ready to leave with her, to go with her wherever she took him.

"I suppose you want to find Giacomo and see if he's the guy your sister left Mace for," she said, figuring someone had to pull them back to earth. If he wasn't going to, she would.

"Jessie . . ." He reached out and brushed a stray lock of hair from her cheek. Then he let his hand drop and turned away. "Yeah. Let's go find him."

THE DRIVE WAS TOO SHORT. She wished she'd had a few more minutes to reflect on things before they reached their destination.

Specifically, she wanted to reflect on the longing she felt whenever she glimpsed his rugged profile, his hands, the sleek lines of his hips and the torment in his eyes. As much as she wished to feel those hands on her again, to kiss his profile and press her hips to his, she wanted even more to learn the truth behind the pain that haunted his eyes. She wanted to know Clint—as a friend or a lover, either way. She just wanted to know him.

Instead, she was stuck showing off her knowledge of Beverly Hills, while Clint sealed himself away from her inside a meditative silence. Her voice sounded strained as she directed him to the street the kid had named. Once they were on it, they had no trouble locating a corner house with a mailbox featuring a rooster.

The circular driveway was jammed with cars, and Clint parked out on the street. Climbing out of the car, they heard a gentle wash of voices emerging from the house. Beverly Hills sounded different from Sunset Strip.

No raucous music here, no shouting, no rumble of traffic along the manicured palm-lined roadways. Everything was refined in this exclusive enclave: the houses, the yards, the sidewalks, even the air.

Clint scanned the street. He seemed to be fighting against a sneer. The rarefied atmosphere of the community had unsettled her the first time she'd visited, but thanks to people like Paul Gaskin, she'd learned that rich kids could be as messed up as poor kids, that they needed social workers and refuges like Rainbow House every bit as much as kids from less privileged families. Sometimes they needed her more.

If his expression was anything to go by, Clint obviously didn't share her sympathy for people with too much. The chip on his shoulder was so big she could practically see him staggering under the weight of it.

"Clint?"

He turned and gave her a dubious look.

"I just want you to remember that the man who lives here may not be the person you're looking for. Mace Bronson said your sister was with someone named Jocko, not Giacomo."

Clint's eyes bored into her, unyielding. If he heard her, he wasn't listening. In the sloping illumination of the post light at the foot of the driveway, he appeared wary, alert, but utterly deaf to her advice.

"You can't bulldoze your way into his house," she valiantly went on. "You have to be polite, and you have to obey the law—which is, this is his home and you haven't got any rights when it comes to questioning him."

He continued to stare at her. A cricket's screech filled the silence between them, and a cynical smile teased one corner of Clint's mouth upward. "Are you done?"

No, she wanted to scream, she wasn't done. She would see him through this encounter with Giacomo, but that would hardly be the end of things. Unless, of course, he forced his own ending upon her.

Not waiting for an answer, he pivoted on his heel and strode up the driveway to the Spanish-style mansion. Windows left and right of the carved oak front door were open; muted laughter and soft rock wafted through the screens.

Clint pressed the doorbell. Jessie heard a musical chime through the windows.

They waited. Breathing deeply, she refused to let her anxiety about Clint affect her. She refused her emotions the attention they demanded, and limited her thoughts to Giacomo and Clint's sister, nothing more.

The door was answered by a young woman in a simple white housedress and apron. Behind her came the distinctive sounds of revelry. "I'm here to see Giacomo," Clint said, his voice ominously steady.

"Do you have an invitation?" the maid asked, her pronunciation spiced by a lilting Mexican accent.

"I don't want to come to his party," Clint explained. "I just want to talk to him for a minute." As he spoke, his gaze darted past the maid to the few chicly dressed party-goers loitering in the marble-tiled entry hall.

"He's very busy," the maid said. "He has a house full of people here."

"I know. I won't take long."

The maid peered curiously at Jessie, then returned her gaze to Clint. "Who are you?"

"Clint McCreary. I'm a lawyer with the Manhattan District Attorney's office in New York City."

She engaged in an inner debate, apparently trying to decide whether she'd be better off to defy Clint or her boss. Clint must have seemed the more formidable of the two, because she yielded to him with a sigh. "I'll tell him you're here, but I won't promise he'll see you." With that, she closed the door.

Clint tossed Jessie a look that seemed to say, *See? I know how to behave.* His polite behavior placated her, but then, he was the sort of man who would always behave courteously toward the hired help. How he might deal with Giacomo was another story.

She herself felt irrelevant, the anonymous observer, his invisible, unheeded conscience. A barbershop quartet of crickets chirped at her from the shrubberies surrounding the brick front porch. She listened to their shrill serenade, and to the tinkle of fine crystal as glasses clinked in the room on the other side of the window nearest her, and to Clint's slow, ominously steady respiration. What would she do if he swung at Giacomo? How would she get him under control if he freaked out?

What would she do if his sister emerged unscathed from this party and docilely left with Clint? How would Jessie cope once Clint's only reason for being in Los Angeles no longer existed?

She'd figure something out. She reminded herself that while Clint might have gotten under her skin, he hadn't gotten into her heart—at least not very far. He hadn't carved his initials into her. Not quite. She would survive his departure because she had to. His departure was even more inevitable than any passion that might exist between them.

The door opened again to reveal a compact, startlingly beautiful man with thick black hair and chiseled chest muscles visible behind the unbuttoned front of his shirt. Jessie tried not to gape at the man's exquisite features. He looked like some of the fashion models she'd seen in high-style magazines, so perfectly constructed he seemed unreal, like a mannequin.

"I am Giacomo," he said with a charming Italian accent. He extended his hand to Clint. "My housekeeper says you wish to speak with me, Mr. McCreary?"

"Yeah. I'm looking for—"

"And you?" Giacomo cut Clint off and turned to Jessie. He lifted her hand to his lips and kissed it. "You are Mrs. McCreary?"

"No. I'm Jessie Gale."

"And you are lovely. A feast for the eyes. I am so pleased to make your acquaintance." He shifted his attention back to Clint. "How may I help you and your lovely companion?"

"I'm looking for my sister."

"Ah, your sister." He winked at Jessie. "You are not his sister?"

"No." She smiled, aware that he was flirting with her.

"So if I make a pass at you, I do not have to worry about the fury of a protective brother?"

"If you make a pass at her," Clint broke in, "you'll have plenty to worry about. Can we talk about my sister?"

"Yes, but not for long. I am hosting a party, and my guests will be wondering where I am. Who is this sister of yours, Mr. McCreary?"

"Her name is Diana McCreary. She arrived in Los Angeles with her boyfriend a couple of weeks ago, and her boyfriend tells me she's run off with you."

"Me? He said such a thing?" Giacomo tossed back his pretty head and laughed.

Jessie was tempted to point out that Diana's boyfriend had said Diana ran off with someone named *Jocko*. But Clint was doing quite well without her assistance, so she kept her mouth shut.

"I understand you're in the music business. So is Diana's boyfriend. I thought your paths might have crossed."

"This town is full of people in the music business, Mr. McCreary. It is full of people with dreams, people with high hopes. I am already a major success in the music business in my native Italy. I know so many people, so many pretty girls, but I do not recall a Diana McCreary among them."

"Maybe she gave you a different name." Clint pulled his photograph of Diana from his wallet and passed it to Giacomo. "Have you ever seen her?"

"Ah, if I had I should not have forgotten. I can see why her brother would worry about her. She is *molta bella*. Very beautiful." He handed the picture back to Clint. "She no doubt has many admirers in this town."

Clint stared down into the deep-set brown eyes of the shorter man. "Sorry to keep you from your party," he said. From his tone, Jessie knew that sorry didn't even remotely describe Clint's emotional state.

"I wish you luck in your visit to our city, Mr. McCreary. *Ciao!*" Sending Jessie a flagrantly lustful smile, Giacomo closed the door.

"What do you think?" she asked Clint after a minute.

"He's lying." Clint touched Jessie's elbow in his chivalrous way, and they descended from the porch to the curved driveway, passing Jaguars and Mercedes convertibles, one Ferrari and one Rolls-Royce en route to Clint's prosaic rental car.

"What makes you think that?" Jessie asked, curious about the workings of his cop-lawyer mind.

"He hears my name once and he memorizes it. He remembers, in the middle of a party, that I'm from out of town. Give me a break. The guy's as phony as a three-dollar bill."

"I thought he was kind of cute," Jessie said, just to rile him.

His hand was on the door handle, but instead of unlocking it he turned to Jessie, scowling. "You thought he was *cute?*"

The devil took hold inside her. "I thought he was gorgeous," she said with a smile. "A bit short, but other than that—"

Clint silenced her with a kiss. A hard, fierce, smothering kiss that shouldn't have turned her on as much as it did. She sank against the side of the car and Clint leaned into her, his body as firm and unyielding as the molded steel at her back. "I haven't forgotten," he whispered.

She hadn't forgotten, either. Before they'd taken this detour to Giacomo's house, they'd been on their way to make love.

But the detour had given her an opportunity to come to her senses. She wasn't sure she should relinquish her sanity now that she'd more or less gotten it back. "Clint, I..."

Her voice dissolved into a moan as he brought his hand to her cheek, as he trailed his fingertips along the edge of her jaw to her throat, and then up to her lips.

"You what?" he asked.

She closed her eyes. All he had to do was kiss her once, touch her once, and her defenses crumbled. "I want you." She sighed.

"You've got me," he vowed, cupping his hand under her chin and lifting her lips to his for another kiss, this one gentle, sweet, as reassuring as possible, given that all his reassurance couldn't change a thing. No matter how much she wanted him, no matter how willingly he gave her what she wanted, he would never be right for her. This would never work.

His lips still caressing hers, he reached around her and opened the door. "Let's go," he murmured.

She was grateful for the chance to sit, given the way his kisses seemed to turn her bones to water. He closed her door and she closed her eyes, reliving the heat and texture of his mouth on hers, the lush desire that swelled within her as his hips met hers.

The metallic click of his door opening jarred her to alertness. She swallowed to steady her voice, and said, "Make a left at the corner."

She piloted him back to Mulholland, and from there to Laurel Canyon Drive, which wound south to Sunset Strip in West Hollywood. She scarcely noticed the stars winking through the stretch of night sky; the towering royal palms and the mansions lining the roads failed to register on her. As they approached the Strip she ignored the bright signs, the billboards and boutiques, the swarms of people hanging out. At any other time, she would be combing the hangers-out for runaways, lost souls, kids who needed her help. But not tonight. Tonight all the people were a blur, citizens of an alien world, a universe irrelevant to her.

Tonight, she had Clint.

With a sudden lurch, he hit the brake. Her seat belt jammed against her stomach as the abrupt halt of the car tossed her around in her seat. "Clint—"

"Damn it," he muttered, yanking on the steering wheel and spinning the car around a corner. "There she is."

"Who? Your sister?"

"The ghost."

Before Jessie could say another word, Clint tore down the road in hot pursuit of . . . a *ghost*?

9

ASA COP, Clint hadn't had to do car chases very often—
in the heart of lower Manhattan, the traffic was so slug-
gish and gridlocked that most perpetrators preferred to
flee on foot. But he knew the moves, the strategies for
how to tail a suspect in a vehicle.

He'd glimpsed the ghost-woman through the windshield of a geriatric Volvo cruising away from the curb
in front of a gourmet ice-cream shop. The driver was a
young man, no one Clint recognized from Bachelor
Arms.

He wasn't going to let her out of his sight this time.

Except...

Except that more than wanting to find out who she
was, more than wanting to locate his half sister, he
wanted to take Jessie home and make love to her.

He had never been pulled in so many directions before. From early childhood, he'd always been able to aim
at a single target, bull's-eye it and move on. His talent lay
not in being able to juggle several things at once, but in
figuring out which thing was most important and jetti-
soning the rest. Clint lived simply, and he got done
whatever needed doing.

Right now one thing needed doing: finding Diana.
Second-most important was tracking down that con-
founded woman with the black hair and the creamy

complexion, and finding out what her game was. Making love with Jessie . . .

The hell with the raven-haired woman, the hell with his empty-headed sister. Making love with Jessie was the only thing that mattered.

He pulled over to the side of the road and let out a long, weary breath. The Volvo vanished around a curve in the road. He let it go.

"A ghost?" Jessie asked quietly.

It sounded so stupid when she said it, he couldn't think of a reply.

"Clint. Look at me."

He didn't want to. He knew if he faced her, she would see how confused he was. A man trying to seduce a woman wasn't going to win points by behaving baffled and indecisive—let alone berserk. He sure wasn't going to win points by telling her he was spooked by an apparition in a mirror in his apartment.

Yet he couldn't *not* look at Jessie. God help her if she labeled him with one of her clinical terms, but when she was beside him it was all but impossible not to stare at her, to lose himself in her breathtaking blue eyes.

They were as beautiful as always, scrutinizing him with profound concern and . . . pity. Cripes. Next thing he knew, she was going to have him committed to some discreet institution for the harmlessly deranged.

"I was going to ask if you were okay," she said, her voice so gentle he wanted to punch something. "But I can see you aren't."

"I'm fine."

"Why don't we go somewhere, get some coffee and talk?"

He didn't want to get coffee. He didn't want to talk. He wanted to haul her into his arms and tear off her clothes, and nibble a path between her breasts, and inhale that innocent baby powder fragrance that clung to her skin. He wanted to slide his tongue farther, down between her legs, until she was writhing and screaming his name in pleasure. He wanted to love her and love her until they collapsed in exhaustion, and then he wanted to sleep all night with her next to him, and wake up and make love with her again.

Coffee wasn't anywhere on his list.

"There's a nice little espresso bar in the next block," she told him.

Swell. A nice little espresso bar. This was heavy-duty California territory, and he wasn't in the mood for it.

But there wasn't much chance of his getting Jessie into his bed at this point, anyway—and he had only himself to blame for that. He might as well play out the scene, go to the nice little espresso bar and see what could be salvaged of the situation.

She pointed the place out to him, and he pulled into a parking space. His heart thumped erratically; he felt restless, ill at ease. How could he explain himself to her when he couldn't even explain himself to himself?

The evening was already much too overloaded. He'd danced with Jessie, felt her body moving against his, felt her arms tight around him, felt her tongue against his lips. If that hadn't been enough to rattle his nervous system, he'd followed it by meeting Diana's new paramour—Clint was convinced Giacomo was the man his nitwit sister had linked up with.

But Clint could deal with him later. Right now, he had to deal with the prospect of drinking coffee-flavored sludge from a teeny-tiny cup while Jessie did a clinical analysis of his dementia.

A skinny man with green hair and a nasal voice greeted them at the café's door and led them to an empty table in the outdoor section, fenced in from the sidewalk and protected from the sky by a striped awning. A candle flickered at the center of the table, offering barely enough light for Clint to read the laminated card listing the café's gourmet coffees and teas. At the bottom, he spotted Irish coffee and felt his spirits lift slightly.

Jessie requested a decaffeinated cappuccino. Once the green-haired waiter gathered the menus and left, Clint was left with nothing to do but look at her. The candle sent a golden radiance up into her face, underlining her chin, the edges of her cheekbones, the tantalizing sculpture of her upper lip.

"Tell me about this ghost," she said.

He measured her tone. Whatever pity she'd harbored earlier seemed to have been replaced by healthy curiosity. "It isn't a ghost," he told her, acknowledging that he had no choice but to tough out the conversation. Jessie was the sort of woman who didn't let a thing go, but pushed and pushed until she got to the bottom of it. He leaned back in the canvas director's chair and tried not to be distracted by how long her eyelashes were. "The people who live in Bachelor Arms *say* there's a ghost living in the building, but I don't believe it."

"Then why did you go driving like a maniac after this ghost you don't believe in? You saw the ghost earlier, too, didn't you?" she accused, a smile of understanding illuminating her face. "This afternoon, when you were about to drop me off at Rainbow House, you saw the ghost and you went tearing off after it."

He couldn't deny it. "I saw a woman who—"

"I wonder if it has something to do with me," Jessie went on, as if he hadn't even spoken. "You keep seeing the ghost when I'm with you."

"I've seen her when I was alone, too," he said, then realized he'd all but admitted he *did* believe in the damned thing. "What I've seen is a person," he corrected himself. "A woman who looks like the ghost."

"How would you know this woman looks like the ghost if you haven't seen the ghost?"

Clint was spared from having to answer by the arrival of the green-haired waiter with two steaming glass mugs of coffee, Jessie's denatured and Clint's enhanced. The waiter served the drinks, smiled, and sashayed away. "The real question," Clint pondered, gazing after the man, "is how can you tell the ghosts from the ghouls in this town?"

"He's making a statement," Jessie rationalized. "I'm sure he feels very glamorous."

"With green hair?"

"Given the droughts we have around here, we can use all the greenery we can get. Now, quit stalling, Clint. Tell me some more about this ghost. Where did you see it when I wasn't with you?"

"Here's the thing," Clint said, leaning forward so no one at the adjacent tables would overhear him discussing something so ludicrous. "I don't think what I saw was actually a ghost. I think it's a woman trying to do a number on me."

Jessie looked concerned. "Why would anyone want to do a number on you? Do you think it has something to do with Diana?"

He shook his head. "It's not *me* specifically. It's some kind of gag. Apparently the last guy who rented my apartment was so freaked by the alleged ghost that he vanished into the night, leaving most of his furniture behind. That's why I was able to luck into a one-month lease. Although maybe luck is the wrong word."

"If you got to live in that magnificent mansion, I'd say it's a good-luck ghost," Jessie said, amusement warring with amazement in her tone.

"It's not a ghost at all," he protested. "It's a woman."

Jessie took a sip of cappuccino, and when she lowered her mug her upper lip wore a film of steamed milk. Clint wanted to kiss it off. When she flicked her tongue over her lip, he wanted to kiss her even more.

But she was laughing. "Okay, so you've got this woman in your apartment, pretending to be a ghost. And you were going to bring me back there tonight? I'm not into threesomes, Clint. I'm a saint, remember?"

He had to admit what he was saying sounded pretty kooky. Still, he couldn't share Jessie's laughter. "The woman's not in my apartment. She was in that Volvo we were chasing. I don't know where she is now."

"Has she ever been in your apartment?"

"Yeah. The first time I saw her."

"Was she floating around? Wearing a white sheet over her head and dragging some clanking chains behind her?"

Jessie was making fun of him. He should have been offended, but he couldn't really blame her. His cockamamy tale deserved ridicule. "She was in a mirror," he said.

"A mirror."

"The mirror comes with the apartment. It's stuck to the wall. It's a big, ugly mother. People claim the ghost lives in the mirror."

"She *lives* in it?" When Clint nodded, Jessie let out another laugh. "Too bad my specialty is *The Wizard of Oz*. This sounds more like *Through the Looking Glass*."

"All right, look." If she was going to turn this into a joke, they could end the discussion right now. "There's no ghost. It's just a mirror. A woman somehow made herself appear in it, and now she's roaming the streets of L.A. I've seen her three times in the city, twice down in the USC neighborhood and then here on the Strip tonight. It's a gag somebody's trying to make me the butt of, that's all."

"That's not all." Jessie stopped laughing, though her smile remained. She watched as Clint took a swig of his Irish coffee. When he lowered the mug, she said, "Maybe the woman you've been seeing around town just looks like the ghost."

"Meaning...?"

"Meaning, there *is* a ghost, and this woman you've seen resembles her."

"*Right.*"

"What did she look like when you saw her in the mirror? Was she wearing the same clothes you've seen her roaming the streets in?"

"No. When I've seen her around town, she looks normal. I couldn't tell what she was wearing in the car tonight, but otherwise, she's been dressed in slacks, shoes, simple jewelry.... You'd see her and not think twice. She looks like a regular human being."

"And in the mirror?"

"She had on a long pale gown. The fabric was a little shiny. What's that material? Satin."

"A pale satin gown."

"There was a lot of mist in the mirror. She sort of appeared out of the mist, in this pale gown, and . . ." He definitely sounded like a nutcase. Another long sip of Irish coffee didn't comfort him. "It's crazy, right?"

"No, it's not crazy. I think it's marvelous." He scowled, and she reached across the table and took his hand. "I believe you, Clint."

"Thanks," he grunted.

"I believe anything's possible."

"Even ghosts?"

"Even ghosts."

He searched her face for a sign that she was merely humoring him, but she looked earnest. Rotating his hand, he wove his fingers through hers and let out a sigh. If she was going to believe him, really believe him, he would tell her the rest of the story. "There's a legend attached to Bachelor Arms," he said. "It's such a big thing they've got a plaque on the wall commemorating it. According to the legend, if you see the ghost in the mirror and she looks straight at you, she'll make either your greatest hope or your greatest fear come true."

Jessie digested this. "Not everyone sees her?"

"No. Just the lucky ones." He put a sarcastic spin on the word *lucky.*

"So, which is it for you, Clint? Your greatest hope or your greatest fear?"

He recalled the hope and fear that had occupied him when he'd first moved into apartment 1-G: the hope that he'd find Diana, the fear that he wouldn't. At the moment, however, he suspected his greatest hope was that, after having shared this dopey yarn with Jessie, she would still be willing to make love with him. His greatest fear was that she'd think he was a fruitcake and tell him to get lost.

She continued to hold his hand, which implied she wasn't quite ready to tell him to get lost.

"I don't know yet," he answered. "I don't know whether I'm going to get the hope or the fear."

"This is really exciting." Her eyes glowed; her cheeks were dimpled. "I hope it's your hope."

"How can you take this stuff seriously?"

"Anything's possible." With her free hand, she lifted her mug and drained it. "I wish I could see your ghost. My greatest hope would be for Rainbow House to become unnecessary."

"Then you'd be out of work."

"I'd find something else to do. But think of how wonderful it would be if teenagers stopped running away from home, if they stopped having a reason to. If kids never got hurt, if they never got abused, if they understood the importance of working out their differences with their families and finishing their schooling. If kids could be safe... I'd like to believe that someday even that might be possible."

Gazing into her eyes, seeing the fierce hope that radiated from them, Clint believed that Jessie believed. He himself knew such optimism wasn't worth the energy invested in it. Kids were always going to go astray. Families were always going to fall apart. Evil was always going to lurk in the earth's dark corners. Safety would always be an illusion.

And yet, to be able to share Jessie's faith in humanity, in the possibility of goodness ...

He envied her positive outlook, even though he couldn't buy into it. He respected her. He admired her.

And he desired her, more than before. More than he thought he'd ever desire anyone. A woman so hopeful, so resplendently optimistic... He wanted her even more than he wanted to believe that life was fair and happy endings were possible.

"Can I ask a favor of you?" she said.

"Sure."

"Will you show me the mirror? I want to see the ghost."

A bark of laughter escaped him. "You want to come to my apartment and look at the mirror?"

"As opposed to ... *oh*." Her face flushed as the implications of her request became clear. "You were planning to bring me to your apartment all along, weren't you?"

"Not to see my mirror."

"Yes, well ..." She averted her eyes. Her cheeks grew even rosier and her hand twitched nervously within his. "I know that was the original idea, but ... but then we took that drive to Giacomo's mansion, and..." She drifted off uncertainly.

She looked so beautiful when she blushed. Which wasn't to say she didn't look beautiful when she wasn't blushing. But her nervousness, her naïveté, her sweet apprehension made him realize how untouched she truly was. He didn't think she was a virgin—she sure as hell didn't kiss like one—but she was untouched by the cruelty of life. Even as she worked with kids who were horribly wounded by it, she remained somehow innocent enough to believe in ghosts and legends and hope.

Clint didn't think he'd ever been that innocent. He'd given up on hope long, long ago. He was a realist, alert to the world's viciousness, prepared for it. Jessie spent her working days saving lost souls, while Clint spent his making sure those irredeemably lost souls got locked up. Experience had taught him what was worth believing in—and it wasn't much.

Yet he couldn't dismiss Jessie. She wasn't a Pollyanna, blithely unaware of what was going on in the real world. She did know how bad things could be—and she believed in ghosts and goodness, in spite of it all.

She believed him, even when he didn't believe himself.

"Okay," he said. "Let's go see the ghost."

WHAT SHE SAW in the mirror was Clint. And herself.

Throughout the brief drive to the pink mansion on Wilshire Boulevard, Jessie tried to unravel the tangled threads of her thoughts. Had she asked to see the mirror because she wanted Clint to make love to her? Or did she really believe the peculiar legend he'd told her about the ghost?

He clearly didn't believe it. Yet the fact that he didn't kiss her, didn't even touch her as he led her up the front walk and inside the building, nodded a greeting to a neighbor who passed them in the hall, and ushered her into his living room implied that seduction wasn't the main thing on his mind.

He brought her directly to the mirror. "There it is," he said.

He hadn't lied when he'd said it was a big, ugly mother. The thing consumed most of one wall, and its frame was grotesquely ornate. Jessie gave it a light tug, but it seemed firmly bolted to the wall.

She stepped back and studied the reflection in the glass. She saw Clint's living room in reverse, the furniture the previous tenant had left behind, the overstuffed sofa, the writing desk, the phone, the chairs, the patterned rug. She saw Clint.

"Where was the ghost when you saw her?" she asked.

In the mirror she saw Clint approach her. "First the mist started spreading across the glass—"

"From the center outward? Or from the top down?"

"I don't remember. I saw something move in it, and the next thing I knew, there was all this mist and she sort of appeared, right in the middle."

Clint's reflection was in the middle of the mirror now, perfectly clear and mist-free. His hair fell back from his face, and his smile was pensive. His shoulders were broad and beckoning, just as they'd been when she'd cuddled with him on the dance floor at Thunder. His eyes, she noticed, were watching her in the mirror as she watched him.

She swallowed. There was no ghost here tonight. Only spirits—the spirit of Clint's passion burning in his eyes as they gazed at her in the glass. The spirit of her own passion, gazing back.

He stepped behind her, his eyes still watching her in the mirror as his lips brushed the edge of her jaw. "You brought me here for this," she whispered to his mirror image.

"I brought you here—" he wrapped his arms around her waist and pulled her back against him "—for whatever you want." His hands folded together like a belt buckle on her belly. "If you want me to take you home, I will. If you want to set up a ghost watch, we'll do that." He moved his thumbs against her solar plexus, sending frantic messages of yearning through her body. "If you want me to kiss you, I'll kiss you."

She couldn't tear her eyes from the mirror, from the tall, strong man looming behind her, sketching deceptively innocent patterns across her midriff with his thumbs. "What do *you* want?" she asked, her voice even more hushed than before.

"Whatever you want, that's what I want," he said.

She knew what he wanted. She could see it in his dark, beautiful eyes. She could see it in her own eyes, in her parted lips, in the way she sank against him, pressing her shoulders into his chest and her bottom into his hips. She wanted to witness the ghost, but the mirror revealed only the truth: that she desired Clint, that merely by wrapping his arms around her he could reduce all her wants to one pulsing need.

His hands moved. She watched them in the mirror as she felt them on her body, sliding up across her T-shirt to her breasts, arching around them and kneading the rounded flesh. Clint watched her watch him, watched her nipples harden, watched his fingers narrow on the small, swollen points and gently pinch them.

She caught her breath, swallowing a moan. His hands abandoned her breasts and traveled back to her belly, and then lower, to her hips, her thighs. She watched in the mirror as one of his hands slid forward and down between her legs, cupping her there, rubbing with increasing pressure until she could no longer stifle her moan.

The feel of his hands on her was overwhelming. Watching made it almost unbearable, and she closed her eyes.

"Open them," he murmured.

She did. He was still watching her in the mirror, watching his own hands rise to the waistband of her jeans and pluck open the button. She shuddered but forced herself to continue watching as he inched down the zipper, pushed down the jeans and her panties, and slid his hand between her legs again.

"Clint . . ." She was so inflamed, so damp, so eager for his touch. She was shocked by the ease with which his fingers glided over her, parted the swollen folds of skin and entered her.

More than shocked, she was intrigued—so intrigued she no longer wished to look away. In the mirror she saw a new aspect of herself, too aroused to be shy, too excited to be embarrassed by the sight of what Clint was doing to her, the sight of herself surrendering to the exquisite hunger he had awakened within her.

"Clint . . ." Her hips moved with his hand, her knees flexing, her bottom shifting against him.

He groaned. She realized then that he was, if anything, more aroused by the scene in the mirror than she was. His breath was uneven, his eyes even darker, and his erection dug into the small of her back. She reached behind herself and groped for him, anxious to touch him as he was touching her.

With his free hand he hastily opened his jeans, then guided her hand inside his briefs. As she closed her fingers around the thick, hard shaft he groaned again. "Oh, Jessie . . ."

"It's the mirror," she whispered, observing his response to her touch in the silver surface, his face contorted in pain and pleasure, his hand becoming still against her as he thrust into her palm. "It's the mirror that's bewitched us."

"No," he argued, pulling free and swinging her into his arms. "It's just plain *us*."

A few long strides carried them to the couch. Clint set her down on the plump cushions, then stripped off her shirt, her bra, her jeans and panties. In less than an instant he'd removed his own clothes, as well.

As dazed as she was by the arousal smoldering inside her, she allowed herself a frank perusal of his body as he tossed her clothing onto a nearby chair. His legs were as lanky as she'd known they would be, his chest sleek with lean muscle. Wisps of black hair darkened the skin around his nipples and tapered down to his navel. His abdomen was flat, his thighs taut. Before he settled onto the couch beside her, she let her gaze linger on his erection, rising from a nest of curly hair, physically proclaiming how much he wanted her.

The cushions were barely wide enough for both their bodies, but somehow they fit, Jessie on her back and Clint half on his side, half on top of her. He kissed her so deeply she felt the impact of his kiss throughout her entire body. His tongue stroked, conquered, and his hand mimicked it, stroking down, sliding deep, conquering.

"I'm sorry," he moaned as she wedged her hands between their bodies and traced the supple masculine surface of his chest.

"Sorry?" She wished the word hadn't registered on her. Afterward, she would have plenty to be sorry for, but she didn't want to think about that now.

"For going so fast," he explained. "I want to slow down, but . . . ahh." His voice dissolved into a gasp as Jessie found him again, circled him, glided her hand over his glorious length. "If you do that, I won't . . ."

"Won't what?" She smiled, understanding her power as a woman in a way she'd never understood it before. She was used to getting millionaires to donate money, getting teenagers to listen to her, getting social-service employees to comply with recommendations. But she wasn't used to getting a man to move to her tempo, to yield to her, to cede control merely because she was a desirable woman who could turn him on as much as he turned her on.

"I won't be able to go slow." He shifted, rising higher onto her and sliding one of his legs between hers. She tightened the circle of her fingers around him and he gasped again. "Jess . . ."

"Don't go slow." She realized that he had as much control over her as she did over him. His fingers found her again, chafed and caressed and made her whimper helplessly. He shimmied down to kiss her breasts, one swift, hard kiss on each nipple, and then he reached over the side of the couch and rummaged in a pocket of his jeans. When he rose back onto her he was holding a wrapped condom.

She might have asked whether he carried one with him all the time, or simply stashed one in his pocket with the express intention of using it tonight. But in all honesty, she didn't care. That in the frenzy of their mutual need, in the blazing desire that refused to let them go slow, he could remember to protect her—it was one of the most generous gestures she could imagine.

And then her imagination shut down, overcome by the reality of Clint's body taking hers. She didn't have to imagine anything, didn't have to dream, didn't have to wonder. The truth made thoughts and dreams irrelevant.

He filled her, he plunged inside her, he gave and took and unlocked her soul by locking himself inside her. He moved gently and tenderly, then wildly, ferociously, surging deeper and deeper into her, drawing more and more from her.

Her body shook, arched, opened completely to him. Her arms clung, her hips undulated, her eyes filled with tears from the intensity of it. She felt his lips brush over hers, the delicacy of his kiss in stark contrast to the increasing fervor of his thrusts. He propped himself above her with one hand; the other skimmed down her side, pausing at her breast and then journeying to her hip and angling her more snugly against him.

She rose toward a peak, raced toward it. Clint thrust harder, urging her closer and closer until the tension broke over her in a deluge of pulsing heat. A moan tore from her throat as the sensations carried her over the edge and down, down through layers of bliss into a dark languor. Above her Clint wrenched, and groaned, and descended to meet her in ecstasy.

A long time later, she heard him let out a ragged breath. She supposed that she would have to start breathing again, too. Her lungs reluctantly stuttered back into operation, and when she inhaled, her breasts pushed up against the smothering weight of his torso.

"I'm crushing you," he said, although he was clearly in no hurry to get off her. She ran her hands up and down the smooth, hot skin of his back and he sighed. "That feels too good," he murmured, propping himself up on his arms and peering down into her face.

"Only you would think it was possible for something to feel *too* good," she teased.

He didn't share her smile. Perhaps he sensed the underlying truth in her words. He wasn't used to things working out, going right, bringing joy. Always, even when he was laughing, when he was kissing her, when he was dancing and joking with her, she sensed the shadows in him.

As he rolled onto his side, resting against the back cushions and holding her so she wouldn't fall off the couch, she almost understood those shadows. Making love with him had felt too good. Too good because she knew he was going to leave her. Too good because no other man had ever pleased her the way Clint had, no other man had known where to touch her, how to touch her, how to bring her to such a pinnacle of sensation— and she doubted any man she would meet once Clint left her would be able to love her as he had. It had felt too good, and she was going to be devastated when he left.

She continued to glide her hand over his side, along the ridge of his shoulder, across his chest and down to his waist. He kissed her brow, the tip of her nose, and sighed again. She wondered if he was thinking what she was thinking: that this too-good moment, this union, this meeting of bodies and souls, was doomed.

Slowly, she extricated herself from his embrace and sat up. The room looked as she'd remembered it: the clunky, comfortable furniture, the small writing table with a card on it—*her* card, she realized, noticing the rainbow arcing across the rectangle—the window with its wrought-iron grille, the patterned rug. The massive mirror.

She stood and crossed to the mirror. A twinge of heat seized her as she recalled the way Clint had allowed her to watch his lovemaking in the glass, the way he'd looked wanting her, the way she'd looked wanting him. His daring foreplay had been too good. Everything about this night was too good.

She shook off her melancholy. Maybe in time she would smile at her memory of the too-good night she'd once had with a too-sexy, too-troubled man. Or maybe she wouldn't simply remember it; maybe she would be haunted by it.

She stared into the mirror and saw Clint in reverse, sprawled out along the couch, observing her. He looked thoughtful, quizzical, sated yet not satisfied.

Turning her back to the mirror, she studied him across the room. His intense gaze swept down her nude body, but she felt no inhibitions. She had already seen him touch her, enter her with his fingers... She'd viewed herself in an astoundingly sensual way. Standing naked in a room with her naked lover's gaze on her seemed perfectly natural.

"Tell me about the ghost," she said.

A line creased his brow as he frowned. "I already told you about her."

"Not *her*," Jessie clarified, dismissing the mirror with a wave. She walked back across the room to the sofa and perched herself carefully on the edge where Clint had shifted his legs to make room for her. Taking his hand in both of hers, she squeezed it tight. "Tell me about *your* ghost, Clint."

10

SHE HAD no right to ask.

She had every right in the world.

For this one night they were lovers. She had seen the shadows shift in his eyes, break apart and float away. She had made them disappear, however briefly. That alone gave her the right to ask.

Her question caused the shadows to return, but she held her ground as firmly as she held his hand. From the moment she'd met Clint she had suspected that his soul was troubled, that he could be saved if only someone cared enough to try. Jessie cared, more than she'd ever cared about anyone before.

The silence in the living room grew oppressive. Clint pushed away from the cushions and sat, then leaned over and scooped up his jeans. She wanted to protest that he shouldn't get dressed. But maybe this was his way of announcing an end to whatever intimacy they'd shared only minutes ago.

He surprised her by tossing the jeans over his arm, standing, and hauling her to her feet. "Let's go to the bedroom," he said. "The bed's bigger than this damned couch."

Relieved that he wasn't about to kick her out, she continued to hold his hand as he collected her clothing from the chair and ushered her past the efficiency kitchen to a small, cozy bedroom that overlooked the rear yard of the house. Leaving the lights off, he threw open a window, and a cool evening breeze accompanied the silver shaft of moonlight into the room.

The bed was wide, with a quaint brass headboard. Clint tossed the clothing onto another chair and pulled Jessie down onto the bed, into his arms. "I know there's nothing to the legend of the mirror," he said. "But it still . . . it kind of spooks me sometimes, looming on the wall like it owns the room."

She cushioned her head against his upper chest and smiled as his arm closed around her shoulders. "I know. It spooked me, too."

"But there's no ghost. You didn't see a ghost, did you?"

"What I saw..." She lifted herself slightly so she could view his face. His roguish smile made her cheeks grow hot. "Let's not talk about what I saw."

He toyed with her braid, springing open the barrette that held it and then unraveling the pale locks of hair. "You're the sexiest woman I've ever known, Jessie. You shouldn't be embarrassed by the way you looked in the mirror."

"I'm not embarrassed. Just a little . . ." She groped for the right word. "I don't know. I'm not usually so . . . immodest."

"Of course not. You're a saint."

She eased out of his arm and sat, raising her knees and wrapping her arms around her shins. "You're evading the question, Clint."

"What question?" he asked. More evasion.

"Your ghosts. Your demons. I know you have them."

"Jessie—"

"Like vans. Why won't you ride in my van?"

He sighed and stared at the ceiling. "I told you. They remind me of doing surveillance."

"So what? What's so terrible about surveillance?"

"And suburban car pools, and . . ." He closed his eyes and cursed.

She took his hand again, gently, knowing her question struck a nerve. She couldn't credit her professional expertise for having stumbled onto this particular ghost of Clint's. She wasn't his social worker. She was his lover, going on instinct, forging ahead because she had to.

"Tell me about it."

"You don't want to know."

"I do, Clint. More than you can imagine."

He stared at her. She had grown accustomed to the dark, and she could make out every angle and plane of his face, every nuance of his expression. It spoke of pain, of sorrow, of emotions that had nothing to do with vans.

"My mother died," he said.

Jessie nodded. She'd figured as much; Diana was his half sister. Perhaps his mother had died in an accident, a crash with a van. Or she'd been run over while crossing a busy street, or—

"The guy who murdered her made his getaway in a van."

Jessie flinched. She hadn't known it was that bad. "I'm sorry, Clint," she murmured, suffering a pang of guilt for having forced him to speak of such a tragedy.

Evidently he wasn't going to accept her apology. She'd torn open a scar, and he had every intention of bleeding on her. "I was seven when she was murdered," he said. "I saw it happen."

"Clint—"

"My real name is John Clinton McCreary. Clinton was her maiden name. John was my father's name, but my mother said she wanted to honor her family. So I was called Clint, just for her."

He paused, waiting for Jessie to interrupt once more, to tell him he didn't have to go on. But the urge to apologize had left her. He *did* have to go on. He'd started this—actually, she supposed, *she'd* started it with her prying—but now that it was in motion, neither of them would be able to rest until he'd told her everything.

She felt his hand relax in hers, and only then did she realize he'd been clenching it. His tension seemed to drain from him, his defensiveness and resentment ebbing. His gaze softened, and although she still saw pain in his eyes, she didn't see the dark agony she'd noticed so many times before.

"My parents were childhood sweethearts. They married young, had me young, and they were saving up to buy a house. The neighborhood was getting rough and they wanted to move out. So my mother worked days and my dad worked nights. She was a secretary. A smart lady."

Jessie nodded, encouraging him to continue.

"We had an apartment on the third floor of an old building. My dad had to go out one afternoon to pick up something at the hardware store. He told me my mother would be home any minute, and I should watch for her from the living room window, and not answer the door or the phone until she got home. I should just sit by the window and watch for her. So I did."

His voice cracked slightly, and he turned to gaze at the ceiling again. "I saw her. She was right at the corner, practically in front of our building. And I saw the guy in the ski mask who snuck up behind her and swiped her purse. And I saw her struggle for a minute, and I saw him shoot her, and yank off her wedding band while she was bleeding to death on the sidewalk. And then his accomplice drove up in a van and they drove off. So you're right, Jessie. I hate vans."

She didn't know what to say. Her social-work training hadn't given her any handy phrases to recite when a man exposed such a deep, unhealed wound. "I'm so sorry," she murmured, hating the inadequacy of her words. "Clint, I'm so sorry."

"My father went off the deep end," he continued, as if she hadn't even spoken. "He felt like it was his fault, maybe he shouldn't have gone out, maybe he could have saved her, something. I don't know. He had— I guess it was a nervous breakdown, although at the time all I was told was that he was upset and couldn't take care of me. I lived with an aunt for a while, but that didn't work out, so this cop took me in. He was the cop assigned to my mother's case. He'd interviewed me a bunch of times, and he and his wife had taken in other foster kids, so I lived with them a while. He was the only father I had for a few years."

"And that's why you became a cop," she guessed.

"He was a good man. What you social workers would call a role model. I was definitely on the road to hell, but he brought me back."

"Your father recovered, didn't he?"

"He came for me when I was twelve. He'd gotten remarried and wanted to take me home."

"You'd never met your stepmother before then?"

"No." Again Clint became engrossed in the ceiling.

"That wasn't a very good way to build a new family," Jessie remarked, once more aware of the inadequacy of her words. She tried to picture a young Clint, rejected, frightened and grief-stricken, suddenly having a strange woman presented to him as his new mother. No doubt his father had only been doing the best he could under desperate circumstances. But his best had clearly been dreadful.

"I hated my stepmother," Clint addressed the ceiling. "I U-turned real fast, started back down the road to hell— and then Diana was born, and she sort of got me back on track."

"Really?" Jessie smiled in spite of herself. "A baby? Your stepmother's baby?"

"She was so innocent," he said, lowering his gaze to Jessie, searching her face as if he wasn't sure she understood. "I swore to myself she was never going to go through what I went through. I was going to save her, and while I was at it I'd save the world, too. You aren't the only person who ever believed it was possible to save the world, Jessie. I was going to do it, too."

"You *have* done it," she told him. "You were a police officer. I'm sure you saved lots of people."

He issued a caustic laugh. "Yeah, right. You arrest a guy, he jives the judge and walks—and spits at you on his way out the door. You try to save someone and find out he's using, or he beats his old lady, or he steals lunch money from schoolchildren, and you wonder, what's the use? Most people aren't worth saving, Jessie. At least in the D.A.'s office, I might be able to put a few more of them behind bars. I sure didn't have much luck cleaning up the streets as a cop. The minute you sweep up one piece of trash, another blows in and takes his place. Sorry, Jessie, but most people aren't worth saving."

"You came to Los Angeles to save your sister," she pointed out.

"I must have been insane to think I could save her. She's tight with that Giacomo character—"

"You don't know that for sure."

"And anyway, you're right. She's eighteen, she's an adult, and no matter how much my folks want her to go home and be their sweet little girl again, it's not going to happen. I don't know why I bothered to come."

"You came because you cared," Jessie suggested. "Because you wanted to try to get her back." *Because fate conspired to allow our paths to cross. Because life contains forces we can't always understand. Like ghosts, like hope and fear. Like love.*

The moonlight played over his face as he studied her. He looked unconvinced. "Did anyone ever tell you you've got your head in the clouds?"

"Everyone," she said with a shrug. "Or they tell me I haven't got my feet on the ground. Most often, they tell me I'm riding a tornado over the rainbow. They say I'm a fool to think I can solve kids' problems by having them click their heels three times and say, 'There's no place like home.'"

She ran her fingers along the thick bones and ridged knuckles that shaped the back of his hand. She recalled the way he fisted his hands when he was angry or tense. Lifting his hand to her lips, she kissed those tense, strong knuckles and wished her kiss alone would be enough to heal him.

"Maybe I'm the one who's insane," she admitted, brushing her lips against his hand again, and watching his eyes grow brighter, his body tauter. "But if you're going to be insane anyway, why not be happy? Why not believe in ghosts, and in the possibility that you can save your sister? Where's the harm in it?"

He opened his mouth and then closed it, rethinking his words. "The more you hope for, the greater the disappointment when your hope doesn't come true."

"Is that your greatest fear, Clint? That your greatest hope won't come true?"

His eyes locked with her for a moment, and then he pulled her down to him. "Right now," he murmured, "you're my greatest fear."

Her? How could she be his greatest fear?

He didn't give her a chance to question him. Turning, he pressed her down into the mattress and silenced all her questions with a kiss.

HE DIDN'T KNOW HOW she'd gotten him to tell her so much. He could have pretended it was some social-worker trick, but one thing Clint had never been good at was lying to himself. When his mother died, he had never told himself that she was just asleep and that if he was really, truly good she would wake up and return to him. Whenever he'd thought about her, he'd been brutally honest: *She's dead. The bad men killed her. She's not coming back.*

When he'd had to move in with his aunt, and she'd promised him that his father would be coming for him soon, he'd known better than to believe her. He hadn't pretended his father was just upset; he'd known the old man was in serious trouble, drinking too much, lashing out, pushing away all forms of comfort. When Clint had taken to staying out late, skipping school, cursing and committing petty vandalism, he'd known what he was doing was wrong. When Sergeant Mullin and his wife had taken him in and said, "You're in trouble, Clint, and we're going to try to get you out of it," Clint hadn't downplayed his plight. He'd been in trouble. No sense lying to himself about it.

Now, he couldn't lie to himself about Jessie's ability to shake loose his secrets, his bitterness, the thirty years of life that had shaped him into the man he was. He hadn't revealed himself to her because she was a good listener, or a professional therapist, or a saver of lost souls. He'd revealed himself because she was a woman, brave and stubborn and relentless. He'd revealed himself because of what he'd seen in the mirror tonight: not a ghost but Jessie, giving herself to him without reservation, without hesitation, without demanding anything more from him than this one night. Like the dreams that had once bewitched him, she had appeared in his mirror and wound up in his arms, her body merging with his, yin to his yang.

Her lips were swollen from his kisses. Her fingers danced across the scruff of his neck, graceful and gentle. Her body, surging beneath him, was all soft curves and hollows, velvet skin and quivering responses. She was more than the California golden girl of his fantasies. She was Jessie, strong and hot and powerful.

He drew his hands down her body, needing to touch every square inch of her skin, every surface, every swell and slope. When he flattened his palm against her abdomen she sighed, and when he curved his hand around her hip she gasped. When he lowered his mouth to her breast and took the sweet, tight bud of her nipple between his teeth she whimpered with pleasure.

For this moment he didn't fear her. Her power flowed into him, making him feel indomitable, able to transform her the way she transformed him. As hard as he was, she was soft, damp, pliant as he stroked and spread her legs, as he slid down to kneel between her thighs and kiss her belly.

"Clint..."

Her voice was less than a whisper, less than a breath in the moonlit room. He skimmed his lips lower, wedging his hands beneath her and lifting her to his mouth.

"Clint..."

She gathered fistfuls of blanket and arched against him, her heels digging into the mattress, her thighs trembling as he feasted on her. She lurched and twisted beneath him, she strained and cried out, and her throbbing release made him even harder.

Drawing himself up beside her, he reached into the bedside drawer for a condom, his hands fumbling because he wanted her so much. Her quiet gasps were like a wanton song in his ears; the movement of her body next to him drew all sensation down to his groin, rendering his fingers numb, too clumsy to tear the damned foil open.

He felt her hands on his, easing the condom from his grip and deftly opening the envelope. She smiled and reached for him, sliding her hand up and down and all around before she unrolled the sheath over him.

Protection was a necessity. He'd never before thought of it as a turn-on. But whatever Jessie was doing to him, it made his entire body sizzle like an ignited fuse burning toward a stick of dynamite.

"We could skip the rest," he joked, his tone hoarse as she tightened her grip on him, making the fuse burn faster. "This feels great."

"I'll make you feel even better." She pushed him down on his back and rose onto him, straddling his hips.

He had promised himself that he would slow down this time, make it last, make her come again and again before he let go. But when she lowered herself around him, when her body absorbed him in its heavenly heat, and her breasts brushed tantalizingly against his chest, and her hair spilled over his face, he doubted he would last a minute.

"I take it back," he groaned, unable to stop gazing at her beautiful face above his, her glistening eyes, her teeth nipping at her lower lip. "You're not a saint."

She smiled. "What am I?"

"A woman. A wizard." She moved her hips in a lazy circle and he nearly lost it. Clamping his hands on her bottom, he tried to slow her down. "Jessie . . ."

She closed her eyes, bit harder on her lip and let him take over. He thrust hard, observing the subtle tension tightening her throat, the flush of passion washing her cheeks. She threw back her head and emitted a sound, the sort of purr a tigress might make. Shivering, she sank onto him, her body convulsing around him, squeezing and teasing and fraying what little control he had.

Damn. He couldn't hold back. Not with his words, not with his body. Not with Jessie Gale.

She was a wizard, all right, carrying him over the rainbow and into her own magical universe. With a helpless groan, he went.

"I STILL WANT TO SEE that ghost," she said.

Morning sunlight streamed through the window. Jessie sat at the small table in the dining alcove, dressed in her T-shirt and panties. She was sitting cross-legged on the seat of the chair, which made her look like a little girl—except for those long legs, and the rise of her breasts under the loose cotton of her shirt, and the narrowness of her waist, and the fullness of her hips.

Waking up to find her in his bed had been like a miracle, a dream come true. He hadn't expected last night's bliss to last into the morning—he never expected anything good to last for long. But Jessie had stayed the night and awakened with him. Sleepy and warm, he'd made love to her the way he had always intended to, taking his time, drawing her along, leading her—and himself—to the verge and then backing off, and then bringing them both to the verge again, until they were delirious with longing. They'd peaked together, perfectly, two forces merging into one.

Now she sat, looking girlish with her golden hair framing her fresh-scrubbed face and her body hidden by the baggy T-shirt. Cradling a mug of coffee, she stared at the mirror on the opposite wall. "I'm sure she's in there. I want to see her."

He found himself wondering whether the mirror was the real reason she'd come home with him last night. What a line, he thought sourly; instead of etchings, a man could invite a woman up to see his haunted mirror.

Most women wouldn't fall for such a corny come-on. Most women were a lot more pragmatic than Jessie.

"There's no ghost," he said.

"The world is full of ghosts, Clint. They're everywhere. Even if you can't see them, they're there. And I'll bet there's one in your mirror." She gazed intently at the silver glass. "What's your theory? Do you think there's a camera planted behind the mirror?"

"It would have to be a monitor," he pointed out. High-tech gadgetry had never been his forte, but as a cop he'd had banks and convenience stores on his beat, and he'd learned the way a closed-circuit TV worked. "The camera would be somewhere else, with the woman, maybe in another apartment. The mirror would be a one-way glass, so if the light hit it a certain way it would turn into a window. You could hide a monitor in there—"

"Why would anyone go to so much trouble?"

Clint shrugged.

"And the mirror is attached to the wall. Wouldn't there have to be a hole behind it for the monitor?"

"The wall behind the mirror backs on another apartment. Maybe that's where the hole is."

"Why don't you knock on your neighbor's door and ask to have a look inside?"

He said nothing. The idea of paying his next-door neighbor a call had occurred to him, but he'd refrained. If there *wasn't* a hole on the other side of the wall, he would have to contend with the possibility that the appearance of the woman in his mirror had no logical explanation.

"I've been busy," he finally said, just to get Jessie to stop staring accusingly at him. "I've had other things on my mind. I'm in town to find my sister. I don't have time for a ghost."

Jessie took a quick sip of coffee and turned back to the mirror, but not before he'd glimpsed the dejection in her eyes. She must have taken his words to mean he had no time for her, either.

It was true. He *didn't* have time for the lovely woman in his apartment. He didn't have time to be wanting her the way he did, wanting her so much he would be happy just to cross Diana permanently off his list and retire to bed with Jessie for the next hundred years or so. He didn't have time to be feeling what he was feeling.

Especially since, whatever he was feeling, it didn't fit into the world of an ex-cop assistant D.A. from New York City—a man who put no stock in ghosts or optimism or all the other things Jessie believed in.

He carried his mug into the kitchen for a refill, and used the separation from her to collect his thoughts. Maybe he was blowing things out of proportion. She was more fixated on his ghost than on him; maybe that actually was the main reason she'd spent the night with him. Sex was all well and good, but in the morning, his mirror took center stage.

Maybe she was focused on the mirror because she couldn't focus on Clint. Maybe she preferred his mirror to him because she knew the mirror would never hurt her.

Clint's life was guided by the principle that things weren't meant to work out. Jessie had understood from the start that this couldn't be a long-term affair. Love had no part in it. It was merely a result of attraction, desire, insatiable lust, a craving as imperative as his need for oxygen and water and the warm, shimmering sunshine that filled his apartment.

Damn. He didn't want to crave the Southern California sun. Back in New York, November and sunlight were mutually exclusive.

Back in New York, there weren't ghosts in mirrors, or outdoor espresso bars in the winter, or beaches where a person could swim year-round. Back in New York, the clouds hung low and the air stung with cold, and there was no one like Jessie to throw his emotions into a tailspin.

He carried his refilled mug back to the table. Jessie had crossed the room to study the mirror up close. He observed the streamlined muscles of her calves and those alluring knees of hers, and remembered how her legs had felt around his waist, holding him inside her.

He swore to himself once more that last night hadn't been about love. But it had been about more than sex. It had been about trust. Need. Hope and fear.

His hope no longer seemed to revolve around finding Diana. His fear no longer related to the prospect of losing her to a heavy-metal thug or a slick Beverly Hills stud.

Jessie *was* his greatest fear. She knew him too well. She knew what made him tick, what made him withdraw, what made him want to protect himself. She might not have known the details until he'd told her last night, but she'd known enough, even without his telling her about his nightmarish childhood.

And if she'd been right about him, maybe she was right about the ghost, too. Which was an even more frightening thought.

She turned from the mirror. Her expression was wistful. He wished he could tell her what she wanted to hear: that she was right, that there was no harm in expecting the best from life; that in spite of all that was sordid and rotten in the world, a person could still be hopeful; that every storm left a rainbow in its wake. He wished he could tell her that he would stay in California because she was there, and the possibility of spending another night with her, and another, and another until the end of time was too tempting to resist. He wished he could tell her he believed what she believed.

He wished he could tell her he believed in the ghost.

"She won't show herself to me," Jessie said quietly. "I guess my greatest hope won't come true."

The stark sorrow in her eyes sliced through him like a blade, lacerating his soul. He wanted to make her greatest hope come true, but he couldn't. He couldn't stay in L.A. forever, couldn't change his philosophy for her, couldn't turn into something he wasn't. Not even for Jessie.

"I'll take you home," he said.

Nodding, she turned back to the mirror, searching its glossy surface for what Clint couldn't give her.

11

"GARY? It's Jessie Gale."

"Jessie!" Gary Balducci emoted over the phone. "Love of my life! Have you finally decided to elope with me?"

She faked a laugh. She wasn't in the mood for Gary's harmless flirting, but her dismal spirits weren't his problem. "I've got a question for you, Gary. Have you ever heard of someone named Giacomo?"

"Giacomo? Wasn't he the artist who created all those long, skinny sculptures?"

"That's Giacometti. This is Giacomo. He has just the one name. Supposedly he's a successful rock star in Italy."

"Giacomo?" Gary meditated for a minute. "Never heard of him. Is he with a U.S. label?"

"I don't know. I don't know anything about him, except that he owns a home in Beverly Hills. Not one of the biggest mansions in town, but not one of the smallest, either. He's young and handsome, and you don't get to live in a mansion like that unless you've got access to a hefty bank account."

"Giacomo." Gary ruminated some more. "I wish I could help you, Jessie. There's nothing I love more than helping you. I've got this wild fantasy that if I help you enough, you'll do a striptease for me on my desk."

"Gary..."

"Which is neither here nor there," he breezed along. "Speaking of how helpful I am, did you find Mace Bronson?"

"Yes, thanks to you. I'm eternally grateful."

"Not grateful enough to run off to Maui with me, though."

"Maui?" She forced herself to play along. Gary was so good-natured and obliging, he deserved better than grouchiness from her. "I thought you were going to drag me to Las Vegas. Maui's a whole different story."

"Great. I'll buy the tickets, you buy the sunscreen." He paused, then reverted to the original subject of her call. "I swear I can't think of anyone named Giacomo. If he was in the business, I would have heard of him. You know I know everybody who's anybody, but I don't know him—which leads me to the conclusion that he's nobody."

"I figured as much. I've already spoken to an associate of mine at MTV. He drew a blank, too."

"It could be the guy makes his money peripherally. There are a lot of ways a person can get rich in the music business. And not all of them are legitimate."

"I know." She sighed. "I appreciate your help, Gary."

"There you go, appreciating me again," he groused. "I hate being appreciated. I'd rather be blanketed in whipped cream and licked clean by a blond social worker."

"I'm sure you would." Her laughter was genuine, but short-lived. As soon as she said goodbye to Gary and hung up, desolation dropped its cold, damp mantle onto her again.

She was the haunted one now; she was the one beset by shadows. Last night she'd learned the truth about Clint. She'd seen the goodness inside him, the open, trusting benevolence he kept hidden beneath layers of protective armor. She'd discovered how tender he could be, how easy to reach once she'd found a crack in his shield and slipped through.

But he refused to acknowledge his own goodness. He didn't want to acknowledge it.

The fact that *she'd* acknowledged it was enough to make him consider her his greatest fear. The last thing she wanted was for Clint to be afraid of her. But she was so headstrong, always so sure of herself, positive that she could save anyone, whether or not he wanted saving. She'd pushed and poked and insinuated herself into Clint's most private, painful memories—and now he feared her.

She had only herself to blame.

"Hey, Jessie!" Susan gave a perfunctory knock on Jessie's door before sweeping into the office. "Break out the bubbly. I've got news for you."

"Oh?" Jessie manufactured a smile. "What news?"

"Andrea's going home. She talked to her parents, they told her they loved her, and they've got an airplane ticket waiting for her at LAX."

"Andrea?" Jessie scrambled through her mental files, attempting to come up with an identity.

"You know, that runaway you picked up the other day. The holdout who didn't want to talk. She's talking now. She said she left home because her mother found birth control pills in her bedroom and grounded her for life. There are some serious issues at stake, but I talked to the parents and they're willing to work with a family therapist. Bottom line, they want Andrea home, and she wants to go."

"Great." Jessie heard the lack of enthusiasm in her tone and tried again. "That's wonderful, Susan. You did a fabulous job with her."

"Okay, so what's wrong?" Susan flopped onto the couch, kicked her sneakered feet onto the coffee table and shoved her shaggy hair out of her face.

"Nothing's wrong. It sounds as if things are going well. I wish I *did* have some champagne. You've earned it, Susan."

"Uh-huh." Susan pulled a face. "So, what's wrong?"

Jessie groaned. Just as Susan could wrest a taciturn runaway's story from her, so she was going to keep at Jessie until she wrested the truth from her.

"I'm worried about Diana McCreary," Jessie offered, pleased that it wasn't a lie.

"Diana McCreary?"

"We've got her photo on the board in the entry. She's still AWOL."

"I thought you said she was eighteen. She can take care of herself, can't she?"

"I don't know. She may have taken up with a slimy playboy type named Giacomo."

"Giacomo?" Susan singsonged the name, making it sound ridiculous.

"He's currently residing at an impressive Beverly Hills address. Nobody seems to know quite who he is. I'm afraid Diana might have gotten sucked into something she can't handle. She's lived a sheltered life, according to her brother."

"Bingo," Susan said, perking up. "Let's talk about her brother."

"Why?"

"He's the cop from New York, isn't he?"

Jessie swore under her breath. She didn't want to talk about Clint with anyone. "He isn't a cop," she muttered. "He's a lawyer."

"Ugh. Even worse," Susan joked, curling her lip.

"Don't, okay?" Jessie snapped.

Susan's grin vanished. "Oh, Lord, Jessie—what happened? What did he do to you?"

"Nothing." *Everything.* She recalled every single thing he'd done to her last night, every kiss, every caress, every shocking intimacy...and she recalled every word, every confession, his shockingly intimate revelations about how he'd become the man he was. He'd shown her his ghosts and faced his pain, not because he wanted to but because Jessie refused to let him run away.

His bravery awed her. His ability to resurrect himself from the tragedy of his childhood moved her. And even though her efforts had driven him away, she still wanted to save him.

More than wanted to—she *had* to save him, because if she didn't, he would be lost to her forever. And if she lost him, she would lose a part of herself, as well.

"How could you?" Susan asked, the harsh accusation tempered by her muted tone.

"How could I what?"

"Fall in love with him."

Jessie confirmed Susan's accurate perception with a sigh. "I know, it's not like me," she admitted. "I'm not fickle, Susan. I'm not the kind of person who jumps blindly into love."

"So what happened this time?"

What, indeed? Ever since Clint had dropped her off at her apartment that morning, and kissed her cheek and said goodbye with a finality that wrenched her heart, Jessie had been trying to figure out what had happened.

"There's something about him," she reasoned, plowing through her puzzlement. "Something incredibly honest, and it reached in and grabbed hold of me, and I had to be as honest as he was. It was like—" It was like a ghost in the mirror, like magic and mystery, a force that cut through all the game playing, all the social niceties, all the wooing and cooing and shilly-shallying. It had left Jessie and Clint with nothing but the undeniable truth, a clear image in the silver glass, a reflection of a man and a woman who needed each other so much it frightened Jessie as much as Clint. "I can't explain it," she finished lamely.

"I'll bet he kisses like a dream," Susan guessed.

Jessie allowed herself a sheepish smile. "That, too."

Susan sighed in sympathy. "What happens now?"

"He finds his sister and goes home to New York. Or he *doesn't* find her and he goes home to New York."

"Or . . . he doesn't go home to New York," Susan suggested.

This time it was Jessie's turn to scoff. "He would never stay here in L.A. He's got a job there. . . ." A job he'd had only since August, she reminded herself. "And his family's there. . . ." A father who had abandoned him when he had desperately needed a father, and a stepmother who had been sprung upon him without warning, and a half sister who was currently in California, not in New York. "Anyway, I don't think he likes Los Angeles. He thinks going to the beach in November is weird."

"I thought it was weird when I first moved here," said Susan. "In time I learned how to cope with such hedonistic pleasures. He could learn, too."

Jessie shook her head. "This thing between Clint and me isn't going to work. We both knew that going in. The smartest move for me would be to help him find his sister and then get him out of my life."

Susan appraised her friend thoughtfully. "It's not like you to give up, Jessie. You're a fighter. You wouldn't be able to save souls if you were a quitter."

"The hell with Clint's soul," Jessie said in a sudden flare of anger. "Maybe it's time for me to worry about saving my own soul."

Before Susan could question her further—before Jessie could consider what damage her soul might have suffered—her telephone rang. She took a deep breath to calm herself before answering.

"Hi, Jessie, it's Gary Balducci. Listen, I've got a line on that Giacomo dude."

"Oh?" She almost blurted out that she didn't care, that Giacomo was Clint's problem and she had no interest in helping him solve it. Yet the only way she could solve her own problem with Clint was by getting his problem solved so he could clear out of her life. "What did you hear?" she asked.

"You're not going to like this, sweetheart. He's a pimp."

"What?" Fresh anger seized her, clean, uncomplicated anger that had nothing to do with Clint. As the director of Rainbow House, she'd dealt with pimps far too often. They preyed on runaways—even eighteen-year-old runaways—and exploited the kids Jessie was trying to rescue. As far as she was concerned, pimps were the scum of the earth.

"We're talking high-class. My sources say he supplies women to rock stars. I asked around, and the buzz is, Giacomo was a two-bit singer in Italy, couldn't make enough liras to satisfy his extravagant tastes, so he came to California to flex his pecs and try his luck here. He couldn't sing to save his life, but he attracted groupies with his Mediterranean charm and all that, so he set up shop discreetly."

"Have you talked to musicians who use his girls?"

"None of my artists would speak for attribution. They were doing me a big favor, telling me as much as they did. They don't want a fire-breathing social worker to come after them with poultry shears."

"I understand."

"The deal is, Giacomo's girls are beautiful, healthy and expensive. In this day and age, lots of rockers are leery of bedding down just any old groupie, what with deadly diseases and so on. Giacomo's girls come with guarantees."

"Oh, God." A picture of Clint's sister flashed through Jessie's mind, an adorable dark-eyed Sarah Lawrence freshman looking for excitement and plunging head-long into trouble. If she was as naive as Clint contended, she would unthinkingly believe any line a smooth operator like Giacomo would feed her. He was rich, he was handsome, he had an enchanting Italian accent—and if Diana McCreary could drop out of college and run away with a slug like Mace Bronson, she could certainly leave him for an even more deceitful slug like Giacomo.

"This wasn't what I wanted to hear," she admitted to Gary. "But thanks for the tip. Now I know what I'm dealing with."

"You're not going after him, are you?"

"I'm going after one particular girl."

"I'd tell you to be careful, Jessie, but I know I'd be wasting my breath. Careful isn't your style."

Wasn't that the truth, she thought grimly as she thanked Gary again and hung up. If she were careful, she'd be a salaried employee at a government-run social-service agency, spending her days answering to others, unraveling miles of bureaucratic red tape and welcoming the reward of a regular paycheck. Careful women didn't establish their own shelters in erstwhile frat houses, sponge funds from the city's high-and-mighty, and comb the sidewalks of iffy neighborhoods, looking for kids in trouble.

Careful women didn't fall in love with men who could break their hearts.

All right, so she wasn't careful. Right now, her recklessness had to be applied to saving Diana. She would find the foolish girl, deliver her to her brother and send him back to New York.

Only then could she come to terms with her own feelings. Only with Clint gone from her life would she have a chance of saving herself.

SOME PEOPLE COULD overcome the revelries of the night before better than others.

In the bright light of late morning, the Beverly Hills mansion at the head of the circular driveway looked pristine, a vision of white stucco, rippling red tile, wrought-iron sconces and groomed landscaping. Not a scrap of trash lay in the driveway, not a cigarette butt, not a hint that the place had been swarming with carousers the previous night.

Unlike Giacomo's palatial residence, Clint felt the residue of last night in his body, in his mind and his heart and in places he had no name for. He was bone weary, depleted—yet every time he thought of Jessie his damned glands stirred to life and pumped an overload of hormones into his system. Every time he thought of her smooth skin, her firm breasts, the flavor of her lips and way her body tensed and seethed and climaxed around him...

That was the least of it. The real discomfort, the real misery manifested itself some forty inches higher than his groin, in his brain.

How could she have torn his defenses from him so easily? Why had he told her the miserable story of his life? Why had telling her made him feel better?

One answer presented itself, but that answer had to do with dangerous concepts like love and faith and salvation, powerful needs he wasn't prepared to consider.

Strolling up the walk to the brick porch, he tried to concentrate on the job at hand. Giacomo had recognized Clint's name last night, which implied that he knew something about Diana. Clint was determined to find out what.

He pressed the doorbell. The windows were closed, so he couldn't hear the melodic chime inside. The only sounds he picked up were the distant rumble of a lawn mower—in November? he thought with a scowl—and the yammering of a couple of birds hidden in the foliage of a sprawling oak tree. He wondered if the leaves ever fell from the trees in Southern California. He wondered

if the birds migrated south from here, or if this was south
enough for them.

He wondered how he was going to endure the bitter
weather in New York once he had to leave.

The door opened, and he found himself face-to-face
with the maid who'd answered the door when he'd visited last night. Her dress today was a pastel blue, her
apron white. Her long black hair was braided, the braids
wrapped around her head like Medusa's snakes.

"Yes?" she said.

"I'd like to see Giacomo," Clint announced, praying
the guy was home. If he wasn't, Clint would have to kill
precious time sitting in his car and waiting for him to return.

The maid assessed him, a flicker of recognition
brightening her eyes. He helped her out by identifying
himself. "I'm Clint McCreary. I'd like to talk to Giacomo while he isn't entertaining a million of his closest
friends."

"He's very tired," she informed him. "I don't know if
he can see you right now."

"Tell him I won't take long. Tell him it's very important, and it would be in his best interest to talk to me."
He wondered whether he should remind her that he
worked in the Manhattan D.A.'s office.

Evidently that wouldn't be necessary. "I will tell him
you're here," she relented, then started to close the door.

He wedged his foot against the jamb and eased the
door back open. "Thanks," he said, stepping inside.

She glared up at him but didn't argue. Either she remembered that he was a lawyer or she simply didn't want
to tussle with someone who outweighed her by a good
seventy pounds. "I will tell him you're here," she re-

peated in a tense voice, then turned and scampered up the spiral stairs that rose along the circumference of the circular foyer.

Left alone, Clint did a quick survey of his surroundings. If he hadn't known a party had taken place here last night, he wouldn't have guessed. The black marble floor was polished, the ashtray on the mail table spotless. A glimpse through one arched doorway revealed a massive living room spruced up enough to pose for *Architectural Digest*. Every sofa cushion was in place, every knickknack dusted, every rug centered. Even the potted plants looked freshly washed.

It seemed to Clint that, unless she had an army of workers assisting her on cleanup detail, the maid ought to be even more tired than Giacomo.

"Signor McCreary." Giacomo's mellifluously accented voice reached him from behind.

Clint turned and watched the master of the house descend the last few steps. Giacomo wore a dressing gown of white silk, and matching silk trousers. In his left hand he held a scented black cigarette. His right hand was extended toward Clint.

Clint waited until Giacomo had reached the bottom of the steps—and Clint loomed five inches taller than him—before shaking his hand.

"Forgive me," Giacomo said, indicating his bathrobe with a wave of his left hand that left a sinuous thread of smoke in the air. "I have just arisen from bed. What can I do for you?"

"I'd like to talk to you about my sister," said Clint, not taken in by the guy's pricey sleepwear or his phony charm.

"We talked last night, did we not? You showed me her photograph. A very lovely young woman."

"She's the kind of woman who becomes attached to rock stars. Perhaps you know the type."

"Ahh." Giacomo smiled; his teeth were awfully white. "I do know the type. Many women are the type. Not all as pretty as your sister, alas. Carlotta!" he shouted up the stairs. "I need some coffee! Come," he said to Clint, beckoning him past the gigantic living room and into a smaller sitting room with a view of the backyard's built-in swimming pool. "I must sit," Giacomo explained, sinking into the oversize cushions of a Haitian cotton love seat. "Last night I partied. This morning I pay the price."

Clint was paying that price, too—although he would hardly call last night a party. Unlike Giacomo, Clint wasn't paying with fatigue or a hangover. He was paying with his heart, with the aching emptiness left by Jessie when she'd realized that Clint could never be the man she wanted him to be.

He ruthlessly pushed the thought from his mind, and directed his energies to Giacomo. "What I'm wondering is, maybe you knew my sister but she's moved on to someone else."

"I would have remembered if I knew her," Giacomo said.

"You're famous and popular. I'm sure lots of women swing in and out of your orbit all the time. How can you possibly remember all of them?" Clint figured a guy like Giacomo would take his comments as a compliment, even if Clint didn't think there was anything commendable about a man who couldn't keep track of the women in his life.

Giacomo eyed Clint cagily, as if trying to decide whether to be flattered. "You may be right, my friend. Perhaps she passed through these doors. I have parties, people come and people go. Your sister is a groupie?"

Clint gnashed his teeth together and nodded.

"I have met many groupies in my day, Mr. McCreary. Given my stature as a musical artist in Italy..."

"My sister isn't Italian. She's from New York. Do you have any idea where all these groupies wind up after they're done passing through your doors?"

"How can I remember?" Giacomo gave a blithe shrug. "They come, they go, and always there's another pretty girl to distract me. Surely you know what I mean."

Suppressing the urge to throttle the bastard, Clint nodded. "I need to find Diana," he pressed on. "If I can't find her myself, I'll have to call in the Los Angeles police to help me. Because I'm a D.A., I can bring the police into it." Of course he couldn't, but Giacomo didn't have to know that.

The veiled warning had its intended effect. Giacomo's evenly tanned face grew a few shades paler, and he glanced toward the door. "Carlotta! Bring me my coffee!" He turned back to Clint and smiled unctuously. "There is no need for police, Mr. McCreary. Let us not get carried away."

"I don't want to get carried away," Clint said, struggling to keep his voice low. "What I want is my sister. Beyond that, I don't give a damn how many groupies you've got. I just want my sister, and if I can get her without the assistance of the police, that would suit me fine. Now, can you help me out? Or do I have to take steps?"

"Are you threatening me, Mr. McCreary?"

"Yes."

The door chimes resounded, an arpeggio of bells echoing against the curved walls of the foyer. "Threats will get us nowhere," Giacomo persisted, smiling through gritted teeth.

"I don't agree, *Jack*. I think threats will get us exactly where we need to be."

"I believe it is time for you to go," Giacomo said quietly. He started to rise, then paused. Apparently he heard what Clint heard: a brisk argument between two women in the mansion's entry. One voice was clearly Carlotta's.

The other was Jessie's.

"YES, HE WILL see me," Jessie roared, sidestepping the diminutive housekeeper and striding into the foyer. "Giacomo! Where are you?"

The maid grabbed at Jessie's arm, but she shrugged free. She knew Clint was in the house—she'd seen his car parked in the driveway—but she didn't know whether he knew what Giacomo was. For that matter, she didn't know whether Clint was in danger.

As for herself, she didn't care. She was used to forging into perilous situations, getting what she was after—usually a forsaken child—and departing before things got out of hand. That was exactly what she intended to do with Giacomo. She would get Diana and split.

When she'd driven to Beverly Hills, of course, she hadn't planned on running into Clint. Discovering his car in Giacomo's driveway had momentarily stymied her. What would she do if she saw him? What if the sight of him made her remember all the joy she'd shared with him, and all the pain? How would she save Diana then?

Well, she couldn't save Diana if she was falling apart, so she simply wouldn't fall apart. That Clint couldn't make a commitment, that he couldn't trust her, that what she wanted to give him was more than he wanted to take...

Forget it. Concentrate on Diana. There'll be plenty of time to agonize over Clint when the dust settles.

The scrappy little housekeeper was snatching at Jessie's arm again. Jessie shook loose and stormed into the house, following the sound of men's voices into a small den with a wall of windows. Clint stood facing Giacomo, who watched the doorway warily, anticipating her entrance. In a kimono and trousers of white silk, he looked like an overpriced karate champ.

Ignoring Clint, Jessie threw herself at Giacomo. "You worm! Where is she? Where have you got her hidden?"

Giacomo let out a startled gasp and backed up to stand by Clint, whom he undoubtedly considered much more reasonable than Jessie. "Please—calm yourself. Carlotta! Remove this woman—"

"Don't touch her," Clint growled, sending the housekeeper such a fierce look she shrank back from the doorway. Clamping a hand onto Giacomo's shoulder to hold him in place, he sent Jessie a quizzical look. "What's going on?"

"He's a pimp," she said.

Clint moved so swiftly she didn't have time to scream. He spun Giacomo around, grabbed him under both arms and slammed him into the wall, holding him at Clint's eye level, which left the shorter man's feet kicking and flailing several inches above the floor. "Is that true? Are you a pimp?"

"Put me down!" His usually lustrous voice emerged in a squawk of panic. "Put me down! I shall have you arrested for assault!"

"Sounds like fun," Clint snarled. "Carlotta, go call the cops so he can have me arrested. Meanwhile, you tell me where the hell you've got my sister stashed away."

"Please! Please! Carlotta, no cops!" he shouted after her retreating form.

Clint shoved Giacomo against the wall again, with such force a framed print of a Modigliani nude slipped off its nail and tumbled to the floor. "Where's my sister?"

"No police. Put me down and I'll tell you."

"Tell me and I'll put you down."

Giacomo closed his eyes and spat out a Hollywood address. "You'll find the bitch there. Now let go of me."

Clint yanked his hands away, leaving Giacomo to crumple in a heap on the marble floor. "If you did anything to her," he warned in an ominously quiet voice, "I'll be back here to kill you."

With that, he snagged Jessie's hand and hurried with her out of the house.

12

"GET IN THE VAN," Jessie said.

His eyes were blazing, hotter than the sun burning down from its midday peak. "You go back to the shelter," he argued. "I'll go get Diana."

"Like hell you will," she said. "Get in the van and I'll drive. I know the area—"

"Then I'll follow you."

"Clint, you can't drive. You're practically shaking with rage. Get in the van."

He stared at her for a long, furious minute, and then climbed into the van, slamming the door behind him.

This wasn't a good time for an emotional breakthrough. She hadn't ordered him into her van because she wanted to help him overcome the traumas of his childhood. But she wanted him with her. She didn't trust him behind the wheel of a car—and even more, she didn't trust him not to mess things up royally with Diana once he and Jessie reached the address he had all but beaten out of Giacomo.

He sat facing forward, glowering, his wrath spreading in ever-widening waves to encompass her. Let him resent her; let him hate her. She didn't care.

Steering out of the driveway, she, too, kept her eyes on the road ahead, refusing to acknowledge the tension that filled her in Clint's presence. It was a tension as much physical as emotional. She was painfully aware of his long legs, the spread of his shoulders, his large hands curled into fists on his thighs. His thighs. His hips.

Stop sign, she mouthed, forcing her attention back to the road.

She heard Clint draw in a breath and let it out. She heard him swallow. She heard him curse. "How did you know?"

"That he was a pimp?"

He flinched at the vile word. "Yeah."

"Gary Balducci asked around."

"He deserves a medal."

"He deserves my hand in marriage," she muttered, wishing she could spark some jealousy in Clint. Goading him wasn't a particularly great idea under the circumstances. But she was pretty angry, herself, and not only at Giacomo.

Clint surprised her by taking the gibe seriously. "You should marry Gary. Why don't you?"

"I don't love him," she said simply. Her eyes stung with tears as she completed the statement to herself: *I don't love him—I love you.*

How much easier her life would be if she loved Gary— even if loving him would make her number 1,001 on his roster of girlfriends. How much easier if she loved *anybody* but Clint, a man whose greatest fear was the love of a woman like Jessie.

"It was dangerous, doing what you did," he murmured.

"What? Coercing you into my van?"

He shot her a quick, lethal look, then returned his gaze to the windshield. "Going to Giacomo's house alone."

"You went to his house alone."

"I've had police training."

"Which would have done you a lot of good if he'd pointed a gun at you."

"Even so." He sighed and squinted against the glaring sun. "I'm a man, bigger than him. What would you have done if I wasn't there?"

"I would have found out where Diana was. I would have figured something out."

"He could have hurt you." Clint's voice broke. She glanced at him, and he turned to stare out the side window.

Obviously he cared enough about Jessie to fear for her well-being. Well, of course he cared. He cared a hell of a lot about her. If he didn't, he wouldn't be afraid of her, afraid of everything she stood for and everything she could bring into his life if he let her.

Even if he didn't care, he had that old-fashioned streak of chivalry in him. He was a man who opened doors for women, and helped them in and out of cars. Surely he was also a man who didn't take kindly to the prospect of women getting walloped by pimps.

"In case you haven't figured it out by now," she said, stifling the tremor in her voice, "I don't let fear dictate my life. Yes, I was aware that Giacomo could hurt me. But I knew what had to be done, and I did it. That's the way I am."

"You're never afraid of getting hurt."

"I'm *always* afraid of getting hurt, Clint. I just don't let it stop me."

He twisted in his seat to scrutinize her. Feeling the sting of tears again, she blinked rapidly and pretended to be fascinated by the traffic at the intersection up ahead. She admitted that, for all her fear, for all her fearlessness, nothing had ever hurt as badly as the understanding that Clint was going to leave her.

If only she could have held back with him, if only she *hadn't* done what had to be done, maybe she wouldn't have wound up hurting now.

She pulled her sunglasses from the pocket in the driver's-side door and put them on, taking advantage of the opportunity to swab a stray tear from her cheek. The van was nearing the neighborhood where Giacomo told them they would find Diana, an enclave of middle-class apartments amid the glitter and glamour of the city's showbiz environment. In the distance, looming above the neighborhood, the huge white letters of the famous Hollywood sign towered against the fading autumn green of the hills.

"Clint," she said, determined to make at least one thing go right this morning.

"Yes?" He sounded almost eager.

"I don't want you to jump down Diana's throat when you see her."

He didn't respond. Shielded by her sunglasses, she glanced at him. He continued to study her, absorbing her with his fathomless gray eyes.

"You have to approach her gently. God knows what she's been through."

"I realize that."

"It's important for her to know she isn't going to go through something worse with you."

"Jessie—"

"I mean it, Clint. If you want, I'll handle it."

"She's my sister. If you honestly think I could do something worse to her than that piece of slime—"

"*I* don't. The key is to make sure *she* doesn't." She wove through the side streets, scrutinizing each of the low-standing pastel-hued buildings for the one bearing the address Giacomo had given them. "It's possible the apartment's going to be guarded. Giacomo might not leave his girls unattended."

"I can handle the guard while you get Diana out."

"If that's the way we have to play it." She lowered her gaze to his fists. She would hate for the situation to deteriorate into violence, but she was realistic enough to accept that it might. She was thankful for Clint's presence. "There's the building."

She parked illegally in front of a fire hydrant, figuring the risk of a ticket was worth parking as close to the building's entrance as possible. She and Clint sprang out of the van and hurried to the glass-doored entry.

Inside the vestibule, they scanned the buttons. None bore a label with Giacomo's name.

Clint pressed a button with an Italian-sounding name on it. "Yes?" A woman's voice emerged from the speaker, tinny and distorted.

"Is this Giacomo's apartment?"

"Who?"

"Giacomo."

"I don't know who you're talking about," the woman said.

Clint skimmed down the row of buttons to the next Italian-sounding name. When a man's voice cut through the speaker's static, Clint repeated his question: "Is this Giacomo's apartment?"

"Sorry, no."

Jessie's heart began to pound anxiously. What if Giacomo had given them the wrong address? She and Clint could go to the police with what they knew, but by the time the police got around to taking them seriously, Giacomo could have phoned ahead and had his girls moved—or worse. If she and Clint didn't find Diana fast—

"Is this Giacomo's apartment?" Clint called into the intercom, pressing a button that was unlabeled. "I'm looking for Giacomo's apartment."

A hiss emerged through the speaker, and then a scratchy voice. "Who sent you?"

"Giacomo himself. All I want is Diana McCreary. Do you have her with you?"

No answer. Only the hiss, indicating that whoever was at the other end of the intercom hadn't released his button to disconnect Clint. The line was still open.

"Who are you?" the voice crackled after a minute.

"Clint McCreary. I've come for Diana."

"You got money?"

"I'll get the law if you don't let me in."

"You can't come in. I'll send her downstairs." There was another unbearably long pause, and then, "How do I know you're who you say you are?"

"Diana has a beauty mark on her collarbone. She's got a scar under her chin from falling off a swing in a playground when she was a kid. Why don't you put her on the intercom and let me talk to her?"

Nothing but static. Clint kept his right thumb pressed on the button; his left hand shaped a fist of knuckle and bone, hard enough to smash through the wall if he didn't get satisfaction soon.

Static. Hissing. No sound of a human voice.

Unable to bear watching Clint succumb to fury, Jessie turned toward the glass inner door. On the other side she saw a modern metal staircase, the risers connected to one another only by vertical steel pins and the railing a slanting rod of aluminum. A shadow fell on the upper stairs, and then a foot in a tooled red cowboy boot came into view, and another booted foot, a left and a right, slowly plodding down the steps.

"Clint, look," Jessie whispered.

Still holding the intercom button with his thumb, he glanced over his shoulder as a slight, slouching woman with dark, rippling hair, a delicate chin and eyes as smoky and troubled as Clint's appeared at the bottom of the stairs.

Clint's right hand fell from the intercom panel. He unfurled his fist and instinctively groped for Jessie. She slid her hand against his palm and he closed his fingers tightly around hers.

Diana stared at him through the locked inner door. He stared at her. One corner of her mouth twisted in a wry half smile. He stepped closer to the door. On her side, so did Diana.

He reached for the levered handle as she did. So slowly Jessie wanted to groan with impatience, Diana twisted on the handle. The door inched open and Clint jammed his foot into the opening. Then he shoved his hip against the door, hauled Diana over the threshold and hustled her through the vestibule and outside.

None of them spoke—none of them breathed—until they were locked inside Jessie's van. Only then, as she collapsed on the seat behind Jessie, did Diana speak.

"Clint, Clint, what am I gonna do?"

She started weeping. Blubbering. Bawling. Jessie revved the engine, then directed Clint to the glove compartment. "There's a box of tissues in there. She's going to need them."

He located the tissues and passed them back to his sister, who continued to shake with heartrending sobs. Once they were a few blocks from the apartment, Jessie considered pulling to the side of the road and letting Clint climb into the seat next to Diana. But when Jessie glimpsed him, she saw the stern set of his jaw and realized he was in no mood to comfort his sister.

"I left everything there," Diana wailed. "My clothes, my watch, everything! Oh, God . . ."

Jessie wondered if she'd left her innocence there, but she wasn't about to ask. Clint muttered something about how she ought to be glad she'd gotten out with her freaking life, and Diana subsided in her seat.

Within a half hour they had reached Rainbow House. "Let me get her settled inside," Jessie suggested, "and then I can drive you back to Beverly Hills to pick up your car."

"Forget the car," he grunted. "I can catch a cab later—assuming the car's still in one piece. For all I know, Giacomo's had it towed to the edge of a cliff and given it a push."

She had thought Clint would be anxious to get the car back—if not to give his sister a chance to unwind, then to guarantee that he wouldn't have to depend on Jessie's van for transportation. But he seemed in no great hurry to climb out of her vehicle. As she squeezed between the front bucket seats to reach Diana, Clint remained where he was, gingerly running his fingers along the padded dashboard, angling his head to study the upholstered ceiling, scrutinizing the cellular phone and the console that separated his seat from Jessie's.

She slid open the side door, tucked Diana within the curve of her arm and helped her down to the sidewalk. Only then did Clint leave the van. He closed all the doors before following Jessie and Diana up the walk to the shelter.

Inside, Jessie led Diana straight down the hall to her office and sat her on the couch. Susan appeared briefly in the open doorway to see if her assistance was required, but Jessie signaled her with a wave that she had everything under control. Susan signaled back that she would be in the TV room if Jessie needed her.

Diana sprawled out on the couch and buried her face in the crook of her arm. Her shoulders shook, and faint, muffled moans arose from the vicinity of her elbow. Jessie located another box of tissues on a shelf and put it within reach of Diana. Straightening up, she turned and found Clint watching her.

"What do we do now?" he asked.

"Wait for her to tire herself out."

He fidgeted with his hands, then shoved them into his pockets. "She looks okay. Healthy, I mean."

"Yes." Jessie realized he was frantic for reassurance. His expression was grave, his earlier anger blended with soul-deep concern for his foolish, thoughtless sister.

At that moment, Jessie knew he needed comfort even more than Diana did. Turning her back on the sniffling young woman, Jessie crossed the office and gathered Clint in her arms. He pulled his hands from his pockets so cautiously she thought her hug might have been a mistake. But once his arms were around her he held her tight, imprisoning her, informing her with the strength and passion of his embrace that he needed her more than ever.

He smelled clean and fresh and male. He felt lean and powerful and achingly familiar. His lips moved against her brow in what could have been a kiss or a plea, or perhaps both.

Jessie longed to kiss him back, to hear his plea and answer it. But she couldn't. He was clinging to her only because he needed her to get him through this crisis. Once Diana stopped crying and a dialogue began, Clint would retreat from Jessie.

With a final hiccup, Diana lifted her head from her arm and stared through watery eyes at the couple on the other side of the office. "Who are you?" she asked Jessie.

"She's the woman who saved your life," Clint muttered, loosening his hold on her.

Jessie refused to leave his side, even as she rotated to face Diana. "My name is Jessie Gale, and I'm the director of this shelter for runaways. It's called Rainbow House. You're safe here."

Diana nodded, pushed herself into a sitting position, and crumpled a wad of tissues to her running nose. After blowing it several times, she lowered the wad and coughed. "So I can stay here?"

"If you want to."

"For how long?"

Clint interceded. "The thought was, maybe you'd get your ass back home."

"I can't do that." She shook her head. "I can't, Clint. They'll kill me."

He stiffened. "Who'll kill you? That creep Giacomo? Mace Bronson? I'll take care of them, Diana. Nobody's going to kill you."

"I meant Mom and Dad," she mumbled, sounding like a small, frightened child.

Clint snorted. "They would do anything to get you back home, Diana. They're crazy with worry about you."

"They won't kill me? Oh, but Clint—if they found out—"

He inhaled deeply. Jessie could feel the tension rising in him. "What is it that they might find out?" he asked, his voice soft but strained. "How far did this thing go, Diana?"

"You won't tell?"

"I don't know what there is to tell." He looked to Jessie, seeking help.

"You might need to see a doctor," she pointed out gently. "We can arrange for that here if you don't want your parents to find out. We do encourage you to open the lines of communication with them, but—"

"I don't need a doctor," Diana announced. "I'm fine."

"It would be good to see a doctor because . . ." Jessie sought a delicate phrasing. She didn't want Clint to blow a fuse, but there were things, unpleasant things, that had to be discussed, and he seemed in no hurry to leave the room so the two women could discuss them in private. "If you were working for Giacomo—"

"I never did anything for him," Diana said hotly. "He wanted me to, but I refused. He was just working on me."

"What do you mean, he was working on you?" Clint erupted.

"Trying to get me to be one of his girls. Clint, you've got to understand. He was so nice when I met him. I mean, Mace turned out to be such a loser! Like, nobody wanted his music. He's on an express train to nowhere, and then, like, there we were at this club, and this absolutely gorgeous guy came over and asked if I wanted to lose Mace, and I did want to lose him. You know? Giacomo was rich, and handsome, and so cool, and, like, I had to get away from Mace because he was turning into such a problem." Diana gazed meekly at Clint. "Don't be mad, please?"

"I am mad," he said quietly. "I'm madder than you want to know."

Diana erupted in fresh tears. "Please, Clint, don't say I told you so. Just help me out with Mom and Dad, and I promise, I'll never—"

"Listen up, toots." He strode across the room to the couch and hunkered down in front of Diana. Jessie stood on full alert, prepared to kick him out of the office if he risked demolishing his sister when she was in such a fragile state. She watched as he peered up at his sister, as he handed her a fresh tissue and stared into her over-flowing eyes. "I'm mad. Mom and Dad are mad, too. Okay? You ticked a lot of people off. That's a fact, and you're going to have to live with it. Now tell me, did Giacomo make you sleep with men for money?"

"I *did* tell you, Clint—he wanted me to, but . . ."

"Did you have sex with men for money?"

"No."

"I'm not God. This isn't Judgment Day. Jessie needs to know whether she should get a doctor in here to exam-ine you."

Diana gazed past him at Jessie. "I didn't do it. He wanted me to, but I refused. I think he was starting to get really P-O-ed about it, too."

Clint tucked his thumb under Diana's chin and steered her gaze back to him. "Do you know what pimps do when their girls don't obey them?"

"Don't be a cop, Clint."

"I'm not being a cop. I'm being your brother, who was scared witless about you and who wants you to under-stand what could have happened to you. I've dealt with pimps before, and I've dealt with prostitutes. Pimps don't get P-O-ed. They beat up their girls. They force them to do things. They rape them, Diana. Do you understand what kind of trouble you were in?"

Jessie held herself back. She should have known that Clint would deal with his sister the only way he knew how: with brutal honesty. He was coming down mighty hard on the girl, but his stern attitude seemed to bring out her strength. Jessie saw no hint that Diana was ready to crumble.

She did seem a little shaky, sighing and letting her shoulders slump. "Do Dad and Mom understand what kind of trouble I was in?"

"No. They still think you're hanging out with Mace Bronson."

"How much do they have to know?" Again she looked past Clint to Jessie. "They think I'm smart. I can't bear to let them know what a jerk I am."

Jessie hated to come across as a know-it-all social worker, but she felt a little professionalism would clarify things. "What matters, Diana, is not so much what *could* have happened to you, as long as you're aware of how risky your choices were. What really matters is for you to figure out why you made those choices, what drove you to drop out of school and defy your family. If you were bored, or unhappy, or dissatisfied with your classes, or if you felt pressured by your parents to be something you don't want to be . . . You've got to get to the root of it so you can work out the underlying issues. You can't change your life until you figure out how you got to where you are, and why, and what direction you want to travel from this point on."

Diana nodded. So, Jessie noticed, did Clint.

"What I think you ought to do right now, Diana, is give your parents a call and let them know you're safe. You don't have to tell them any more than that if you don't want, but I'm sure they'd love to hear your voice. If you'd like, you can use my phone. I'll give you some privacy." She gestured toward the phone on her desk, then started toward the door. "Clint?"

"Let him stay," Diana pleaded. "Maybe he could, like, talk to them first, break the ice or something?"

"If that's what you want," Jessie said. Her gaze shuttled between Clint and Diana, and then she turned and left, hoping that the McCreary family would be able to establish a peace they could all live with.

Once they did, Clint was going to take his sister home. He was going to go back to New York, back to being the reserved, brooding man he'd been when he came to Los Angeles. But if at least one thing came out right, if one disaster ended happily, maybe Jessie wouldn't have to give up her optimism. Maybe a ghost would appear for her someday, and make her greatest hope come true.

Although once Clint left, she had no idea what she would ever want to hope for.

HE FOUND HER on the front porch, watching the swarms of students strolling along the sidewalks near the university campus. She sat on the top step, her feet resting two steps below her, her elbows perched on her knees and her chin propped in her hands.

He sat down next to her. She glanced at him but said nothing. If she was the sort of woman given to histrionics, he would have searched her eyes for tears. But they were dry, blue and clear and much too knowing.

"Hey, Wizard," he murmured.

"How's Diana?"

"Exhausted. One of your colleagues fixed a bed for her upstairs. She wanted to take a nap."

"Did she talk to your parents?"

"Yeah. She told them she wanted to come home, and they said hallelujah."

"Good." Jessie turned back to the street and settled her chin in her hands once more.

He sat less than an inch from her on the step. He wished he could close the distance between them, but it was the widest, coldest inch of space in the universe. Her beautiful shoulders were hunched, her chest arched so he could barely see the fullness of her breasts. Her lips were pressed into a straight, implacable line.

"I talked to the folks, too," he said.

"Oh?"

"I told them..." He sighed. "I told them something really awful happened."

She flickered a glance his way.

"I told them I went to the beach in November and loved it."

Pink flooded her cheeks and she lowered her gaze. "Well," she mumbled, "fancy that."

"It wasn't just because of what happened between us when we were there," he said. "Although I loved that, too. But...I loved being able to walk barefoot in the sand at this time of year. And to drive around with my windows open, and to smell flowers and hear birds singing this close to winter. I told them I liked L.A."

"And you haven't even visited Disneyland yet," she said dryly.

"I want to. I want to go with you."

Again she looked at him, curiosity laced with something else in her gaze: trust. Distrust. Uncertainty.

"You said it's more fun if you go with someone. We could even..." He forced out the words. "We could even go in the van if we had to. I like the beach but not the van, Jessie. But..." He wished she would smile, nod, give him the merest hint that she understood what he was telling her.

But this smart, insightful woman, this sexy, sassy social worker who knew him better than he knew himself wasn't catching on. "Where exactly is this conversation going, Clint? Are you saying you want to stay on in town for a few weeks, and you'd like an escort? If that's what you want—"

"That's not what I want." The hell with the inch that separated them like a chasm, a canyon, a no-man's-land. He slid closer, until their hips were touching, and looped his arm around her. "I want to change my life," he said, waiting for a spasm of fear to grab hold of him. It was such a momentous thing to want, bigger and scarier than merely wanting a woman. Simply putting his feelings into words frightened him.

But the want was greater than the fear.

He wanted Jessie. And he knew he couldn't have her unless he was willing to see things her way. She would never be able to love him unless he learned to go barefoot in the sand in November, and to accept that while life could be cruel and capricious it could also be warm and friendly and full of passion.

"You want to change your life," she echoed, sounding mystified, intrigued . . . almost as hopeful as he felt.

"You said it yourself," he reminded her. "A person can't change until he figures out how he got to where he is. You helped me figure that out, Jess. I didn't even know I wanted to change, but you helped me figure out that there are other directions I could be traveling."

Her eyes changed, growing softer, brighter, impossibly bluer. Her lips curved upward in a hesitant smile. "What direction do you want to be traveling, Clint?"

"Over the rainbow?" He bowed and kissed her lips. "Will you take me there?"

"You're already there," she murmured, sliding her hand around his neck and pulling his face to her for another, deeper kiss.

Many minutes later, he came up for air. Jessie's lips were damp and sweet and full, and the satisfied sigh she emitted turned him on as much as the kiss had. Her eyes, dreamy with desire, gradually grew clear and sharp as she studied his face in the afternoon light. "Am I still your greatest fear?" she asked.

"Yeah." He laughed, then shook his head. "No. But my greatest fear came true."

"What was your greatest fear?"

"That I'd lose my way of living. That someone like you would come along and kick the props out from under me."

"You shouldn't be afraid of that, Clint. You should be thrilled." She gave him a smug grin. "Admit it—I'm the best thing that ever happened to you."

"You are," he agreed, then returned her smile. "Maybe it wasn't my greatest fear that came true. Maybe it was my greatest hope. I don't know."

"Do you believe in the ghost now?"

He rolled his eyes and laughed. "No. But you still do, don't you?"

"If you asked me to spend the night with you again, Clint, I'd do it for the mirror. I want to see that ghost."

"You'd do it for the mirror," he muttered. "I'm insulted." He mulled over her words and shrugged, refusing to let her teasing rile him. "What the hell—I'll take what I can get, however I can get it. Will you spend the night with me?"

"Maybe."

"And tomorrow night. And the day after. And the day after that."

She struck a contemplative pose. "I might."

"You know, Jessie, if you want to see the damned ghost, she probably lives in this neighborhood. She could be somewhere in that crowd right now." He waved toward a flock of students congregated near the corner, chattering, straddling bikes and executing spins on their Rollerblades.

"We'll find your ghost," Jessie promised. "I believe in her. And deep in your heart, Clint, you do, too."

"Not a chance," he argued, and then bowed and kissed her once more. Maybe he believed in the ghost, maybe he didn't. Maybe he believed the legend, maybe not.

But the ghost didn't matter. What mattered was that he believed in Jessie, in her kiss, in her power to save a lost soul.

Jessie Gale's faith had become his, and he believed.

* * * * *

Coming up in BACHELOR ARMS

*Racked by guilt over a car accident,
Morgan Delacourt insists on helping the woman
he injured. Hope Henley isn't looking for
charity—except she is strangely drawn to the
building of Bachelor Arms and to Morgan
Delacourt. It's as if their paths were fated to
cross. But Bachelor Arms is no stranger to
tragedy. . . . Is history about to repeat itself?*

*Enjoy the romantic and moving conclusion to
the legend of Bachelor Arms
in Judith Arnold's captivating
TIMELESS LOVE (December 1995, #565)*

Believe the legend. . . .

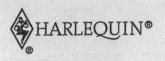

HARLEQUIN®

CHRISTMAS ROGUES

is giving you everything 🎣 **you want on**
your Christmas list this year:

- ☑ -great romance stories
- ☑ -award-winning authors
- ☑ -a FREE gift promotion
- ☑ -an abundance of Christmas cheer

This November, not only can you join ANITA MILLS,
PATRICIA POTTER and MIRANDA JARRETT
for exciting, heartwarming Christmas stories
about roguish men and the women who tame
them—but you can also receive a FREE gold-tone
necklace. (Details inside all copies of
Christmas Rogues.)

CHRISTMAS ROGUES—romance reading at its
best—only from HARLEQUIN BOOKS!

Available in November wherever
Harlequin books are sold.

BACHELOR ARMS

MOVE OVER, MELROSE PLACE

Come live and love in L.A. with the tenants of Bachelor Arms. Enjoy a year's worth of wonderful love stories and meet colorful neighbors you'll bump into again and again.

From Judith Arnold, bestselling author of over thirty-five novels, comes the conclusion to the legend of Bachelor Arms. Whenever a resident sees "the lady in the mirror," his or her life is changed and no one's more so than Clint McCreary's. Or Hope Henley, who looks exactly like the mysterious woman. Don't miss Judith Arnold's captivating:

#561 THE LADY IN THE MIRROR (November 1995)

#565 TIMELESS LOVE (December 1995)

Believe the legend...

HARLEQUIN® *Temptation*

HARLEQUIN®
Temptation

Secret Fantasies

Do you have a secret fantasy?

Holly Morris does. All she'd ever wanted was to live
happily ever after with the man she loved. But a tragic
accident shattered that dream. Or had it? Craig Ford
strongly reminds her of her former lover. He has the
same expressions, the same gestures...and the same
memories. Is he her fantasy come to life? Find out in
#566, LOOK INTO MY EYES by Glenda Sanders,
available in December 1995.

Everybody has a secret fantasy. And you'll find them
all in Temptation's exciting yearlong miniseries,
Secret Fantasies. Throughout 1995, one book each
month focuses on the hero and heroine's innermost
romantic desires....

SF-12

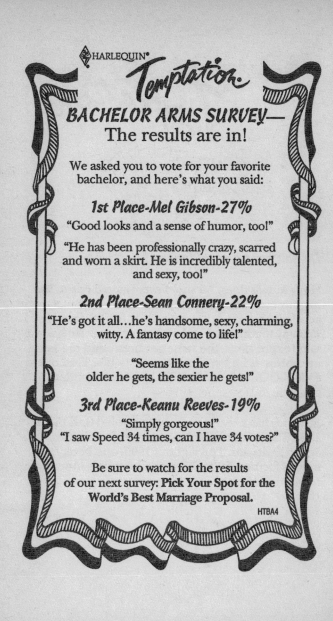

HARLEQUIN®

Temptation.

BACHELOR ARMS SURVEY—
The results are in!

We asked you to vote for your favorite bachelor, and here's what you said:

1st Place-Mel Gibson-27%

"Good looks and a sense of humor, too!"

"He has been professionally crazy, scarred and worn a skirt. He is incredibly talented, and sexy, too!"

2nd Place-Sean Connery-22%

"He's got it all…he's handsome, sexy, charming, witty. A fantasy come to life!"

"Seems like the older he gets, the sexier he gets!"

3rd Place-Keanu Reeves-19%

"Simply gorgeous!"
"I saw Speed 34 times, can I have 34 votes?"

Be sure to watch for the results of our next survey: **Pick Your Spot for the World's Best Marriage Proposal.**

HTBA4

HARLEQUIN PRESENTS®

Don't be late for the wedding!

Be sure to make a date in your diary for the happy event—
the sixth in our tantalizing new selection of stories...

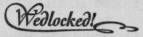

Bonded in matrimony, torn by desire...

Coming next month:

THE YULETIDE BRIDE by Mary Lyons
(Harlequin Presents #1781)

From the celebrated author of *Dark and Dangerous*

A Christmas wedding should be the most romantic of
occasions. But when Max asked Amber to be his
Yuletide Bride, romance was the last thing on his mind....
Because all Max really wanted was his daughter, and he
knew that marrying Amber was the only way he'd get
close to their child!

Available in December, wherever Harlequin books are sold.